SOMEONE HAS TO TELL THE STORIES

SOMEONE HAS TO TELL THE STORIES

Pat Gould

iUniverse, Inc.
New York Lincoln Shanghai

SOMEONE HAS TO TELL THE STORIES

iUniverse books may be ordered through booksellers or by contacting:

iUniverse
2021 Pine Lake Road, Suite 100
Lincoln, NE 68512
www.iuniverse.com
1-800-Authors (1-800-288-4677)

ISBN-13: 978-0-595-39564-4 (pbk)
ISBN-13: 978-0-595-83967-4 (ebk)
ISBN-10: 0-595-39564-3 (pbk)
ISBN-10: 0-595-83967-3 (ebk)

Printed in the United States of America

I have been blessed in my life to have had so many wonderful people be a part of it. Of course, my parents have had a great impact. My siblings have also brought out the best (and worst) of me. Schoolmates and fellow scouts have also had a tremendous effect. I also should mention the many wonderful Cub and Boy Scout leaders that have helped set the direction of my life.

A special thank you must go to a dear friend, Kathy Messbarger, who graciously edited my work with great compassion and professionalism. Without her this would be just a bunch of disjoint words on paper.

The images for the cover of this book are my son's Cub Scout shirts. I appreciate that Grant and Jared allowed me to use them.

With all these wonderful people in mind there is indeed one person that should be recognized over all the rest. That would be my wife, Diane. Without her patience and support I would never have been able to have had the experiences I have had. Her encouragement during the writing of this book was unwavering. She is now, and has always been, my greatest supporter in anything that I have done.

So I dedicate this book to her. That one person in this world that makes me whole.

Contents

INTRODUCTION

I am a Cubber. That is what the early Cub Scout Leaders were called. I am currently serving in my eighth year. During that time I have been a Tiger Adult Partner, Tiger Den Coach, Tiger Den Leader, Assistant Den Leader, Den Leader, Webelos Den Leader, Cubmaster, and Committee Chair. In addition I have been Blue & Gold Chair, Fundraising Chair, Day Camp Leader, and coordinator for numerous events such as Pinewood Derby, Christmas Caroling, Family Camping, and many, many more.

The reason I tell you this is to give you a perspective of just what areas I have had to learn about and grow into. Although I am an Eagle Scout of over 40 years, these challenges have indeed been greater than anything they threw at me during my Scouting years. Since becoming a leader, I have often thought that the main purpose of reaching Eagle was to prepare me for being a leader in Cubbing (another old term).

My oldest son is closing out his third year of Boy Scouts. He is currently a Life Scout and seems quite on track to reach Scouting's highest rank. My youngest is flourishing in his Bear Den with all his buddies. Learning about knives, ropes and all those wonderful things a third grader gets really excited about. I was blessed to have sons just far enough apart that they have gone through Cubbing back to back. Many families have two Cubs at once so they have familiarity with the program the second time through. My great fortune is that I truly get to experience the ENTIRE trip twice.

As I shared the experience with my older son I was in awe of the power of the program. First, I had to understand that there even was one. There was no way I could have understood this as a boy because I was just having too much fun to be bogged down with the details. As I attended training for all the positions in which I have served I strived to take the information they gave me and apply it to my specific group. I have recently finished the fieldwork for my Wood Badge. I will never forget when the Scoutmaster quoted Powell by saying, "Scouting is a game with a purpose." Following that he said, "Let the game begin." That's just what a Cub wants to hear. Let's play a game and have some fun. That is just what we are doing.

This book is a gathering of stories that I feel compelled to share. We all have heard "life lesson" type phrases that we are supposed to learn from. All these wonderful beatitudes just don't make up for reality. What I am sharing with you are stories based on actual events that have happened to me along this wonderful trail of being a Cubber. Some of these stories are events that happened earlier in my life that came back to me as a result of my experiences as a Cubber.

So this little offering is for you, the Cub Scout Leader. That amazing Den Leader who is fretting every week about what they need to get done in this week's meeting AND make sure the records get posted accurately AND don't forget about collecting dues AND push that fundraiser one more time AND help Johnnie find his neckerchief slide, again AND listen to that "concerned" parent about the treatment of their son AND get to the committee meeting to get another to do list from the Pack leadership AND go get that list done AND invest time in their son. This is my tribute to you, the Cubber, who leads our youth with the purest of hearts.

After all, it is for the kids isn't it? So be a kid. Sit back and enjoy reading your stories. I say your stories because I don't believe these experiences are much different than those of any other Cubber. I encourage you to reminisce about the times you have had with your Cubbies and my prayer is that you are more joyous and thankful for doing so.

Yours In Cubbing,
Pat Gould

HOW IMPORTANT ARE THESE AWARD THINGS?

Once in a while the adults get together for some special activity. Our council had just one of these events and it was my natural desire to attend. It is fun to listen to the stories that leaders tell. It is also a great opportunity to learn from them so you don't make the same mistakes.

This was quite an affair and many spouses attended with the leaders. One woman in particular that I met, had three sons who earned their Eagle badges in the late 50s to early 60s. This was very special to me as my mother also had three Eagle Scout sons. I could indeed see her sons accomplishments by viewing her collection of mothers' pins that she wore proudly.

This lady's husband was Cubmaster for many years. The month their youngest earned his Lion they were one pin short. If you have ever served as Cubmaster then you know if anyone is going to go without, it is your son and your family. As the months passed by something unexpected happened. The Lion rank was discontinued to make way for the Webelos program. When they went to replace the pin they were no longer available.

After hearing her tell this story I knew that I could help. Since I am also a collector of memorabilia I do my best to help those who are missing some award from their past. I got her address and a few days later I sent her the memento that made her collection complete.

I received an incredible Thank You note from her letting me know how special it was to have her mother's pins finally complete. What made me feel even better was that a few days later I got a note from her husband thanking me for taking off the heat that had been on him for so many years. It is amazing just how important these baubles are to the boys AND parents.

TEACH TEACHERS

I have concluded that our major objective as Scout leaders is to "teach teachers how to teach teachers how to teach". During the Cubbing phase we are the source of knowledge and instructor of skills for these fine young lads. As these boys move on to the Boy Scout phase, it is their job to take over these roles for the younger Scouts.

While attending Cub Scout day camp with my younger son, we were accompanied by my older son. He is the Den Chief for his younger brother's Den. He has developed a relationship with many of the boys from the Pack. As the third day of our adventure was progressing, I couldn't help but notice just how effective my older son was with these young Cubs. His patience was incredible and his ability to "get to their level" was extraordinary.

I wondered if I was the only one that had noticed. As the boys and their families prepared to have our family dinner at the Day Camp site, we asked a blessing for the food and one of the parents requested that everyone thank the Den Chiefs for their fine work. As I asked each of them by name to stand they were greeted with applause. Of course, a leader cannot show favorites, so I held my son until last. It was an absolute joy when they gave him a standing ovation.

Day Camp is an exhausting time, for leaders, parents and Cubs. After we cleaned our area and returned home my mind was racing with thoughts of what I needed to be prepared for on our last day. As I made my notes the "ovation" event struck me one more time. I was truly moved to tears (actually I was sobbing uncontrollably) as the realization hit me that my son really "gets it".

Yes indeed, I was very proud of my son's actions during the week. What is of even more importance to me is that I look forward to the day when my son comes to the same realization as I did. He did a wonderful job teaching these boys and I knew it. When the time comes for one of those younger boys to take on the role as a teacher, I want to be there to see the look on my son's face when he sees the fruits of his labors.

Teachers affect eternity; they can never tell where their influence stops.

LITTLE MIRACLES

As Den Leaders we struggle weekly to prepare our program for the meeting, fret over collecting some sort of money (dues, fundraisers, etc.), update the advancement records, scrounge for supplies, and on and on and on. All too often we get so wrapped up in our efforts that we just don't take enough time to observe the results.

We keep our focus on the rank advancement. Within our Pack we strive for the boys to achieve this wonderful goal in time for our Blue and Gold banquet in February. Starting in late August or September means that we must go through months of activities before we get there. Obviously the boys are rewarded along the way with some sort of bead or pin to show those little accomplishments, but what is in it for us?

In order to maintain my sanity I have discovered a way to help myself see that progress. Every meeting I look for "little miracles" happening. It may be as simple as seeing that young Cub tie a knot that he had been struggling with for weeks. Or, it could be just how perfect the entire Den makes their Cub Scout Sign during opening ceremonies.

Probably the most amazing of these events is when I see boys working together to finish their task. Anyone that has had more than two boys in their Den knows that the dynamics of the personalities within their Den is one of the most challenging aspects. You have to make sure that the aggressive "A" types don't overrun the more timid "B" types. My initial response to this was simply to separate them. In reality, this is the easy way out.

Making sure they can ALL work together is what we must accomplish. Keeping them apart may seem easier for us, however it is robbing these boys of the opportunity to grow and learn from each other. Every boy has something to offer every other boy and if we don't give them the opportunity to share it we are stealing from ALL of them.

One particular boy in one of my Dens was VERY aggressive. He was extremely intelligent however none of the boys want to be with him because he was so domineering. When I discussed this with the Den Chief for the Den, he made the comment that the other boys just don't trust him. When I asked him why that is, his response was very insightful. "Maybe he doesn't trust them either". What a brilliant observation. He gave me what I needed to work on the situation.

During our next few meetings we had activities that forced the boys to trust each other. One meeting was dividing up the task into parts so that each boy had a part of the whole. It developed in them an understanding of just how important every one was to the group. If we took away just one part (ANY PART) there was no chance of success.

Another was more of a physical nature. As part of first aid training they learn to make a stretcher out of two poles and a blanket. I made sure that our aggressive, untrusting boy was the injured person. I already knew the rest of the boys would be comfortable. Their friend wasn't in a position to be aggressive. The look on the "victim's" face was almost fear in the beginning. As they carried him across the line it had changed to one of joy and appreciation.

This one little event indeed changed how the boys related to each other. There was a much greater level of trust between each other. It turned out to be a "little miracle" with huge results.

SOMEONE IS GOING TO SEE IT

If you have been a Den Leader for more than one meeting, you probably have had a parent not support their son 100% in the Cubbing Program. Having seen so many wonderful things as boys have new experiences, I simply try to offer what I know to be true. Their son is going to do things for the first time; many, many times in their life.

Of course we all are so excited with those first sounds, first steps and first words. But there are so many others that I have greatly embraced. Going through the first "quiet" night and who can forget the first "dry" night? It is so wonderful as a boy becomes his own person. These little steps along the way are really great milestones in my life as a parent. As one who has done a few loads of laundry, I cannot tell you how excited I was the first time I did not have to use prewash on my son's shirt to remove who knows what kind of food stain.

I also look to many in the future as well. Academic and sports accomplishments will indeed come along with new social experiences. Then to see them starting their life on their own, with their spouse and their children (ah ha! I'm back in Cubbing again.).

For that reluctant parent, they need to understand the power of the "firsts" that are happening now in their son's life. It is indeed a time of self-discovery. That moment when they see the results of trying something for the first time. It is absolutely fantastic to see the look on their face when they KNOW that they can do something they never could before.

On one of our Webelos campouts every boy was assigned meal duties. At each meal they had to do the food preparation, cooking or cleanup. On Sunday morning it was one special boy's turn to cook the French toast. The first few were suitable for a leader to eat. One leader commented to me that he had never had "blackened" French toast before. With encouragement and praise he got much better at it. By the time he was done he had developed into quite a cook. They were turning out just fantastic.

As the cooks and I sat down to eat our meals, we were discussing how much they enjoyed their experience. I asked the French toast boy what he was thinking and he said, "Mr. Gould, that is the first thing I have ever cooked in my life.". I felt blessed to have witnessed this "first time" event in his life.

As misfortune would have it, neither of his parents was there to see this inaugural event. As soon as the opportunity presented itself I shared the experience with his mother so she could appreciate the significance of what happened. I was not prepared for the response I received. As a result of his experience she too received a "first time" gift from her son. Shortly after the campout he volunteered to cook breakfast for the family. It was the "first time" ever she had not needed to cook the family meal. Although this boy did not continue on to Boy Scouts, his mother tells me he is still a wonder in the kitchen. And I saw him cook his first meal.

EVERYONE IS A LEADER

One of the fathers in my older son's Den is an Eagle Scout and over the years we have become friends. At the beginning of the first year of Webelos his son transferred into my Den along with another boy. This boy wasn't new to me as he was in the same Tiger Den but ended up in another Den when we had to split the large group into smaller ones.

It was difficult to deal with at first. The dynamics of the boys before they arrived were quite good. They knew how to have fun and they knew when it was time to work. The best thing was the size of the group matched with the individuals in the group did not create situations where the boys splintered. Nor was their major competition for the "spotlight". This had changed.

When Powell began Cubs, he referred to Dens as Sixes. That is because his ideal size for a group at this age was six boys. What we refer to as a Denner was called a Sixer. I have had a Den of six and it was like heaven. My wonderful wife was a Den Leader of 15 and during that time she always seemed stressed to me.

This Den had now grown to 12. It was as though Sir Baden Powell himself was smiling over me as I watched this well-oiled machine of 10 fracture into two smaller groups. It was devastating to see it happen right before my eyes. No matter how I teamed up the boys, the results just weren't as effective as they had been.

For the first time in this Den's history I instituted a Conduct Candle. As a brief description for those who may not know of this tactic, you simply light a candle at the beginning of a meeting. If "conduct" is an issue, the offender blows out the candle. Once the candle has been completely burned up (usually 3 months or so), a special event is held like bowling, pizza, or just games.

Remember my Eagle friend? Well, I am sure there was more of his son's DNA on that candle than from anyone else. My friend was not at all of the meetings so he didn't see all of this; however his wife was usually there when her son was given the task of snuffing the flame. I could see this troubled her and decided to discuss this with my friend.

We have always been candid with each other as Eagle Scouts will be. He shared with me that she wanted her son to be a leader. Don't we all. I am sure she was at the meeting when the boys were reminded that to become an effective leader you must learn to be a positive follower. That is what I was trying to get through to her son.

In this boy's case it was never going to work. He was already a leader. The other boys looked to him for direction. My attempts to make this boy take a step back were futile. He knew that I was troubled and during his "Den Leader conference" in order to earn his Webelos we had a small exchange. He understood what I was asking him to do, however it was hard for him to let go. My next statement hit home when I said, "You will always be a leader—either a good one or a bad one."

Now it was all in his lap and he knew it. He did indeed earn his Arrow Of Light and bridged into Boy Scouts. He has had some problems in his Troop that has warranted discipline. As I watched him walk into "that room" where he was to meet he said, "I wasn't a good leader this time, was I?" He didn't expect an answer and I couldn't have given him one without tearing up.

WHO BRINGS YOU BACK?

As I told you in the beginning, I am in my eighth year as a leader in the Cub movement. For anyone who has attended several Roundtables, you know that the newness of this experience wears off after a couple of years. Training can be another one of those less than momentous events as well.

It was very apparent to me that attending these sessions for 10 YEARS was going to absolutely bore me to tears. Of course I could just say that I've done all that so I don't need to do it any more. Many people do that you know. But that wasn't going to demonstrate much leadership to those new leaders in our Pack that truly needed to gain what is offered to them. Oh, what to do?

Our Cub Scout Roundtable Commissioner, whom I will call Margaret, is a marvelous woman. She has GIVEN her time to this wonderful movement for decades. What truly amazes me about her is that she still has the passion for it. She has a wonderful smile on her face whenever she is delivering the message. A true inspiration if there ever was one.

As I shared my dilemma with her she only had one question, "Why don't you join our staff?" Boy, is she good. How could I tell her no? What excuse could I give? Was it going to cost me another hour a week? She had me and she knew it AND I knew that she knew it AND she knew that I knew that she knew it. Subsequent conversations with her over the past couple of years have revealed that she felt that I could make a good addition to the staff long before it happened. She was just patient enough for me to be ready for it.

The kids truly keep me excited about Cubbing when I am working at the Den or Pack level. It was when I start hanging out with those "adults" that it got tiring. Not any more. Now I just hang around Margaret. She is just a kid at heart. Just wants to have fun. Just like me.

I found mine, now you go and find yours. I am pretty sure that mine could be yours too. You have to have someone that keeps bringing you back to the basics of the movement. Someone that epitomizes just what this thing is all about. Once you have yours don't ever let go. That is until you are ready to be one yourself. Even then I counsel against it because you will always need to have that base you can go home to when the conditions are too great to bear.

YOU WEREN'T READY TO LEARN THAT

Many years ago I was dispatched to another city for my work. Our mission was to prepare a presentation for a potential client. There indeed was a team of us working on this project. That included someone who I will refer to as a "kid". I refer to him with that term not in a negative sense, but rather only in reference to our relative ages.

One of my specific tasks was to work with one of the newer graphics applications. Because I was unfamiliar with the software, the "kid" gave me some pointers to get me started. I worked rather late into the night moving diligently towards the objective while struggling with this new tool. I accomplished a great deal, however I knew that it was not complete and was somewhat dissatisfied with the results.

As is my nature, I arrived early the next morning to continue my efforts. As I finished my third cup of coffee, the "kid" approached me and asked how it was going. I reviewed some of my work and explained to him that there were some things that I really wanted to do and told him that I wished the application could do some specific things.

He then responded that what I wanted to do could indeed be done and he showed me exactly what I wanted to accomplish. After his quick tutorial I was excited about what could be done next. As I recalled our previous days "lesson" I knew he had not detailed these steps to me and I inquired, "Why didn't you teach me that yesterday?" His response, "You weren't ready to learn that yesterday".

What an insightful response from the "kid". As we work with Cubs we must continually remind ourselves that they too are "kids". They are in the process of putting their learning building blocks in place. If we teach them how to put on a roof before they learn how to build a foundation the result will not be what it needs to be.

As we give them these foundation tools and knowledge we also need to keep in mind that every boy is unique. The ability to grasp and master concepts and details will be different for each boy. Just because we have put the material before them doesn't mean they "get it". After all, maybe "he isn't' ready to learn that yet".

SO THEY WANT TO QUIT

Any Cub that has been registered for more than, let's say 2 months, has probably wanted to quit. It's their nature. Everything is so new to them that they want to experience it all and they just can't seem to fit it all in. If you have not experienced this in your Den then you are a perfect Den Leader. If you can capture the imagination of every boy, every week, every year then you are indeed amazing.

Admittedly, I am not that good. Some of the boys want to quit. I have tried the parental pressure approach; however some of them are happy to hear it. One more thing they can cross off their list. Although an attempt at bribery was made, that method was quickly abandoned. As I struggled with this one I asked my son why he wanted to go to Den meetings. His response was golden, "Because I want to be with my friends".

That's the ticket (no Wood Badge pun intended). Just make sure he has friends there. I was certain that I didn't know all his friends so I urged him to invite ALL of them to a Den meeting. You can bet that I made sure it was packed with tons of fun and special treats when they came. To my amazement, it worked. He recruited three boys into the Pack.

Now I set the hook. I explained to him that he had displayed great leadership by inviting his friends to join him in such a great program. I also suggested that he encourage them to invite their friends. They did that as well. Our group of 12 Tigers had grown to 32 by the time they moved into 3 separate Bear Dens.

What every boy knew, as he was recognized for his recruiting efforts, was that he had done a wonderful thing. He also understood that as long as their friend was in Cubs, they couldn't quit because that would take away from their leadership. What had an even greater impact was that these "friends" had time to grow together in a positive, controlled environment. As they gained confidence through their efforts TOGETHER, they grew more reliant on each other. After that they can no longer be friends, they are almost brothers. True companions that would never quit on each other.

PEOPLE DON'T CARE HOW MUCH YOU KNOW

As one embarks on this wonderful journey of leadership, it is important to keep in mind that we are dealing with human beings. Although they are of the younger variety, they are still people. Most have similar desires. They want to be with their friends and have some fun.

When a Den is put together there is a good chance that not all the boys know each other. As their experiences unfold you can observe that there are indeed different types of personalities. Some of these boys are very outgoing while others are more reserved. It is very important that each one feels a part of the whole. This can be difficult at times because some boys just aren't very willing to allow others into their lives.

As I said earlier, these boys just want to be with their friends and have some fun. Not every boy is going to warm up to every other boy, so make sure that EVERY boy knows that he has at least one friend in the group. That needs to be you, his Den Leader. One of the best ways to show him that you are his friend is to learn his name and USE IT. Nothing is sweeter to the ear than the sound of one's name, pronounced correctly and vocalized with genuine care.

You may not like everything about a particular boy. His antics may frustrate you. His parents might tick you off from time to time. However, I make sure I find at least one positive thing about him that gives me something to build upon. Remember the saying "If you can't say something nice, don't say anything at all.". Well, instead of being silent, say something nice anyway. Having that one positive thing gives me an area that I can compliment the boy on.

It is crucial to the development of a child to give them balance in their lives. What I mean by that is that they need different activities to allow them to grow in all areas. This may include sports, church, or other social groups. One of the old Scout promotions was "Scouting rounds a boy out". I am confident that many leaders I know adopted this as their personal guide. This is proven by the shape they have taken over the years.

Scouting does indeed give the boy some balance. It is important to recognize his efforts in these other areas as well. Invest the time to find out just what other activities he is involved in. Ask him about what else he does for fun. Find out what his family does together. Inquire about his school life (teachers, girlfriends, etc.). You will be amazed at just what makes this boy tick. In fact, I am confident you will be impressed with his accomplishments outside of Scouting.

Once you begin developing this type of relationship with a boy, he will begin to count you as one of his friends. He may even share things with you that he doesn't share with others. Never breech his trust. Remember that the first point of the Scout Law is that a Scout is Trustworthy. Demonstrate this through your actions and not just your words. In time, he will become a better Scout because: People don't care how much you know until they know how much you care.

BUT I CAN'T DO THAT

D o you recall the first time you tried to tie a bowline or a sheet bend? Maybe it was a simple square knot. How frustrating was it for you? Ropes might be one of your strength areas, but I'll bet there is some skill that was difficult for you to master. You don't have to admit it to me; after all you are the one reading this. And I'm hoping that you are not reading it aloud. Think about it and I'm sure you will think of that one thing that made you say "BUT I CAN'T DO THAT".

If we as adults have a hard time with some things (or many things in my case), then doesn't it make perfect sense that Cubs will be just like us? Each boy will have one or more things that become a roadblock for him. No matter how hard they try, they just can't get it. Or so it seems.

I use knots as an example because it was indeed an area that I knew my Webelos were just not mastering. I realized that this was not going to happen in one or two meetings. This was going to take some practice. So I started the "know the knot" program at every meeting. I would tie a knot and any boy who could identify it would be awarded a special bead. This was helpful but it wasn't enough.

What made it all come together was when we had the Knot Olympics. I allowed every boy to sign up to compete in 3 of 6 knot tying events. The competition was held over a three-week period. Because of the numbers in the Den and the limits I set on the number of events, it was almost a given that every boy would win one of the gold, silver, or bronze awards.

We practiced knots every meeting for 2 months leading up to the competition. Only 5 or 10 minutes, but it was every meeting. When the time came, they all felt ready to be competitive in their event. It was indeed a success. Every boy did indeed win at least one medal. Some placed in all three of their events. One thing was for sure; they were comfortable tying their knot. In future competitions with other Dens and Packs they learned to leverage the "bowline" boy, the "taut line" tot and the "clove-hitch" kid.

I had shared something with the boys before the process started. I wanted to make sure they still remembered before they bridged into Boy Scouts. As I visited with one of the boys I asked him about it and he said he did. In fact he told me that his parents told him that I had misquoted the saying and he had lost some confidence in me. I asked him what his parent's version was and he told me "Any job worth doing is worth doing well". I agreed that his parents had the correct quote.

Absolute joy filled my heart when he went on to say that he thought my "version" was better. When I asked him to repeat my version, he started without any hesitation, "Any job worth doing is worth doing poorly, until you learn to do it well." As an update, he is doing it well as Assistant Senior Patrol Leader in his troop.

DAD STILL HAS HIS GROOVE ON

It was going to be an exciting event, for me at least. My oldest son had earned his Life rank and the anticipation of the Court Of Honor was really getting my blood flowing. As I visited with my son I could tell that he probably had not realized how great this accomplishment was and how hard he and his family had worked to get there.

Since his Cub Scout days I have always required that he "escort" his mother to receive his awards. He has been told many times that this is one way of showing respect to his mother and showing her how much he appreciates her help along the way. Since he started as a Tiger Cub, this would be trip number 12 to receive recognition for his rank. To say the least he has had some practice at this.

At age 13, I had observed that he was indeed maturing in many ways. Of course he was physically maturing as he repeatedly pointed out that he was taller than his dad. He was maturing socially as well. His interests in girls had been growing too. I must say that he is a good-looking young man and I am sure they have interest in him, too.

As is always the case, I reminded him that he needed to come get his mother and escort her to her position of honor. He reminded me that I had already told him this 11 other times. What I shared with him next, however, was something new. I pointed out to him that this gesture was also a public demonstration of respect for womanhood. He looked perplexed so I simply said, "the girls love this kind of stuff". He smiled and said, "So dad still has his groove on", which made me laugh and of course agree.

The festivities proceeded nicely and it was time for his award. When his name was called, he jumped up and almost ran to his mother. He offered his arm and just as she he took it, EVERY female in the crowd let out the coolest sound I had ever heard. They were impressed with his actions and I am sure their sons were as well.

More importantly he was impressed as he commented later on, "you do still have your groove on, don't you?" He already knew the answer. After a little more conversation he also knew that it was something you need to work on every day.

EVERY BOY WANTS A CLOCK

While serving as Cubmaster it was my honor to recognize the achievements of the boys by presenting them with their awards at Pack meetings. What an excellent opportunity to convey to a boy that at least one person is aware of his accomplishments. Scouting is one area that recognizes him for something he has EARNED.

Because not all things are in the control of the Cubmaster, there were times when the award a boy is expecting is not there for him to receive. It really doesn't matter to the boy how this happens. All he knows is that he didn't receive what he earned. In an effort to demonstrate responsibility to the boys, I ALWAYS accepted the blame for error.

One particular incident involved a boy in a Webelos Den. He had earned an activity badge, however his Den Leader had forgotten to turn it in to the awards person. I was made aware of this before the Pack meeting and told the boy I had made the mistake and would indeed correct it the next month.

In order to keep me humble, as fortune would have it the next month, the Scout shop was out of the award. Another acceptance of responsibility for the error was made on my part. Although I could see he was disappointed, he left the stage with a smile on his face knowing that at least one person cared about his award and he just knew he would get it next month.

It would be grand to say that the next month was the one. However, as I gathered the awards to hand out, THE PIN BROKE. Once again I took the heat. This was now becoming an ongoing saga that many people were having fun with. I did my best to let the boy know that I knew this award was important to him and me as well.

I made it my personal mission to insure that the next month was the one for this boy. I even picked up an extra award just to make sure we had it for him. In addition, I felt it was important to make the presentation "extra special" for him. As most Cubbers know, the local hobby/craft store becomes your home away from home. While strolling down the isles I saw a miniature grandfather clock. You know, the ones they use in dollhouses. This would be just perfect.

As the boy came forward to receive his award for the FOURTH time, I could tell by the look on his face that he wasn't counting on it being there for him. He was pleasantly surprised to discover that he was wrong. Not only did he receive his award, he also was given a neckerchief slide made from that grandfather clock. I told him that this was to remind him that although he waited a long time for his award, it was never forgotten. He now serves as Senior Patrol Leader for his troop.

It is funny just what excites a boy. After that meeting I had several of the Cubs ASK me if I could mess up their awards so they could get one of those "cool" neckerchief slides.

YOU NEVER KNOW WHO YOU'RE REACHING

I have been truly blessed with my current Den. I have one Den Chief serving the boys in my charter. He truly is a fine young man and without him things just aren't quite as smooth. Of course I am biased as this lad is my older son, however as he will attest, I don't pass compliments on without merit.

Last year I was triple blessed by having three of them serving this group of ten. As these boys grow older they move on to other positions of leadership within Scouting and in other areas of their life. One of these boys needed to do just that and when it was time to move on he asked my permission if he could give up his position. He received my permission and blessing.

When it was time for him to receive his Eagle, he expressed his desire to have the boys from "his Den" serve as color guards for his opening ceremony. The boys in the Den were excited and it was absolutely the cutest sight to see them honoring their country and their Den Chief as they carried in the flags of our country. They did a fine job.

The program continued on with an absolutely outstanding guest speaker. In addition there were several stories told about this lad's experiences along the Scouting trail. Since I am not involved in his troop I was delighted to hear these tales of his actions and reactions. Sounded just like many boys I have known who have reached the highest rank of Scouting, including me.

After he was presented his Eagle medal, he then presented his parents with their pins to honor them for their help during his journey. They looked absolutely wonderful, full of pride for their son. My mind raced as I pondered just how I would feel when (and if) my son(s) ever get there. Oh what a glorious day that will be.

I was snapped back to the present when I heard my name called by this new Eagle Scout. My eyes were filled with tears as he asked me to come forward and presented me with an Eagle Scout Mentor pin. It was an overwhelming feeling to have him single me out for this honor and I just couldn't help but wonder "Why me?"

Later in the program he offered thanks to those who helped him along the way. Appropriately he showered his parents with honor and praise for their toughness and help. He talked about his Scoutmaster and other leaders in his troop. He also thanked his fellow Scouts who walked the trail with him.

Once again he mentioned my name. This time my eyes were drier and my heart was more receptive to what he was saying. Although he did say that I was the scariest leader he had met, he said "He knows what he is doing." Then it was clear to me. What he saw in me was my passion for the movement. It truly wasn't that I knew what I was doing, but rather that I understood the power of what could be done. I never dreamed he saw this, and that is a good thing.

MAKE THEM PART OF THE LEGACY

An important part of Cubbing, and especially Scouting, is recognizing customs and traditions. It may very well be as a result of our study of Native Americans. I would bet that you could list five things that your Pack or Troop does as a tradition. I can remember many of the traditions we had in my Pack as a boy and have pity on the leader that attempted to skip that part.

These things are important to Cubs. They need a sense of consistency. In addition, they need something to look forward to. When a boy starts Cubs in the first or second grade they have seen a boy receive his Arrow Of Light for several years. As he finally receives the recognition for his accomplishment this tradition is now part of him.

Early in my Cubber days I asked the new committee chair what he wanted his legacy to be for the Pack. After he responded he asked me the same. What I told him then is something I knew would take a decade to complete so I need to keep that one locked away until I know it is done. Since that time I have witnessed many things involving Cubs that have spawned their own legacy.

The boys in our Pack are presented certain items as part of their Pack dues. One of those is their neckerchief. Because that changes every year we "loan" them to the boys and they are replaced the next year. We instruct the boys to put their name at the top and in the center of their neckerchief. This request came from a leader with 15 boys in her Den who I am sure guessed more than once at whose necker (still another old term) was whose.

Now as part of their graduation ceremony, when the boy gets his "new" neckerchief the names of the boys who have worn it before are sometimes read. Some of the boys' names that are there are still in the Pack so that creates some current connections. What is even more special is when a former Cub from our Pack returns to serve as a Den Chief. It is wonderful to see this Scout make a personal connection with the Cub. Now both of them are part of a very unique Cub legacy.

HOW LOUD IS YOUR DO?

The human brain is an amazing thing. It really has no knowledge other than what we feed it. Have you ever touched a hot stove? Who hasn't? Did you ever knowingly do it again? Probably not. After the first time, your brain stored that painful event and it recalls it in very rapid fashion. All of the senses feed the brain. In the case of the stove it is our sense of touch. Around the holidays I know my brain is triggered by the senses of smell and taste.

In the Den setting, one of the most powerful senses on the boys is the sense of hearing. What they hear you saying has a great impact. Because their brain is relatively empty it is like a big bucket that gathers it all in and stores it. Since many of their experiences are new to them they begin to build a foundation of knowledge with these experiences.

As they grow and mature they will have many more experiences and their observation skills will become sharpened. There will be times when there is conflict with what their brain has already stored as truth. A parent may tell their child that hitting is wrong, and then they are spanked for some bad deed. Isn't that conflict?

When a boy recites the Cub Scout Promise he is making a commitment in many areas of his life. They are all important. Duty to God and Country come first and as such one would believe that they are the most important. Generally, I agree with that perspective. However, it can be somewhat difficult for a child to appreciate the ultimate impact in these areas of their lives.

What they can easily understand is to "help other people". Something they may struggle with is just how to do it. In order to help others, you have to know what their need is. When a classmate drops their book or glove it is easy for them to know that the right thing to do is pick it up and return it to their friend. Other needs may not be so apparent.

The elementary school that my sons attend has a program that provides an opportunity to serve children. Once a month, parents (especially dads) get to read to the kids in their child's class. I started participating when my youngest was in Kindergarten. As the year went by I realized just how much these children NEEDED someone to read to them. I was confident that other than their teacher, we were probably the only adults that ever read to many of them.

I made a commitment to myself that I would continue to do my best to help satisfy this need. I now read to my son's third grade class. In addition, I still read to the classes of his Kindergarten, first and second grade teachers. They gave him the wonderful building blocks, which he is using to continue his education. It was clear to me that the right thing to do was to pay them back.

As you can imagine, I have now seen the faces of dozens of children during these sessions. My "why" was to help other people, students, and teachers. That's it, nothing more. How I do it is to make sure I share something that is both fun and educational. My heart is so full when I see the look on their faces as I reach the door to their classroom. It is clear that they look forward to my visits.

As a result of these sessions two things have come about that I need to share. One of my duties is to man the Pack's recruiting table at the back to school night. It makes the job much easier when many of the boys from last year's Kindergarten class already know me and introduce me to their parents. The parents often comment that their son has talked about me in their homes. Since I read "The Little Cub Scout" to them every year this is not totally unexpected.

The second outcome has been a very pleasant surprise. When you ask children what their favorite part of their school day, most will tell you recess. Sometimes weather prevents them from being able to have it outside. Many choose to take some quiet time on these days either reading or doing some craft. On one of these dreary days I needed to drop something off at the school. As I passed the library I saw a girl that I recognized from a couple of years earlier. Although she is in the third grade now she was reading to some younger students.

I don't ever remember telling any of these kids that they should read to others. In fact, I am confident that I never told them that they should. But kids are observant and they often recall early experiences in their life. To her credit she simply remembered a positive experience and wanted to share it.

Telling a kid to do something sometimes works. Demonstrating to them what should be done almost always works. It reminds me of the saying "What you do speaks so loudly that what you say I cannot hear."

How loud is your do?

PAIN IS WEAKNESS LEAVING THE BODY

I heard this phrase while watching a late night talk show host one evening. He made the statement as he was talking with one of his guests about an injury they had incurred. As I do so often, I try to apply what I see and hear to my Cubbing efforts. This one was so profound to me that I knew it was not going to be an exception.

Change can be painful. We are set in our ways and we really don't want to change. In order to do so we have to stretch ourselves. We have to move out of our comfort zone. It can also be seen as we watch these boys grow when they struggle with new challenges. It is painful for them to not have immediate success at something.

What is important to keep in mind is that we are helping them get stronger. I am sure you have heard the expression "no pain, no gain". In order for them to get stronger they must go through some difficult times. They will not value their accomplishments if they are too easy. Experiencing difficulty is what makes them a better person.

The next time you see that young lad going through some pain while working towards his goal, watch closely. I develop a mental picture of the "weakness" bugs leaving his body and mind. It has become so real to me that I can almost see these creatures falling to the floor as the boy moves forward. Sometimes I even go over near the boy and stomp on them so they won't ever bother him again.

WHAT STATE ARE YOU FROM?

I am from Missouri. Those of us on the West side of the state usually pronounce the end with a long "e", while those to the East usually pronounce it "uh". Now I really didn't mean to pose the question as a geographical reference. What I really want you to consider is something a little more abstract.

As a Den Leader we are usually in a state of confusion and bewilderment. We are constantly asking ourselves: What in the world have I gotten myself into? What should I be doing next? Will this work with my Den? And other questions of a similar nature. There are also times when we are in a state of awe as to the great power this program has on boys.

I strive to operate Den meetings so that it can be described as "organized chaos". If the boys are SAFE, having fun, and learn something, I consider the meeting generally to be a success. In order for it to be a complete success, every boy needs to feel successful. Of course they will fail at times as we all do. It is most important that they achieve something that they can attach a good feeling to.

I just love to recall knot-tying episodes. Probably the main reason for this is that this is the one area that was nearly my downfall to reach Eagle. I had a dickens of a time mastering them all. If it hadn't been for a couple of very close buddies in the Troop and my Scoutmaster, I never would have gained enough confidence to pass the test.

Failure is a state of mind. Success is a state of being. What state are you from?

ARE YOU ONE OF THE 5,000?

I was blessed to have met a very special man while working on a project many, many years ago. Our job was to integrate two systems for one of our clients. We worked well together and both of us had a very strong respect for the other's abilities.

As is true with any computer-based system, we had the opportunity to work many late nights together. Working out the kinks was very challenging. At times we were frustrated, however, most of our time together was enjoyable, and we had an opportunity to exchange stories about our personal and professional lives.

Although we were both long time employees, this was the first time we worked together and subsequently the only time. I was truly impressed with his dedication to the task and the precision with which he worked. He was an amazing technician and a very likable person. He was just a great guy.

After several days with limited accomplishments, we finally began to make greater strides towards our goal. We both applied our knowledge and skill to the best of our ability. As we approached the end of the first week, it was obvious that we had done what we set out to do. We were pleased with the results and so was the client. It was indeed a job well done.

As a reward for our efforts, we decided to go out to dinner the last night that we were together. Our conversation drifted from topic to topic. We did share some personal insights, but most of the talk was about work-related experiences. I gained a tremendous respect for him as he shared just how he approached his challenges and overcame them.

The feeling must have been mutual as he made the statement to me "You must be one of the 5,000." Of course I had no idea what he was talking about so I urged him to explain. His belief was that there are only 5,000 people in the entire country that really hold everything together. He felt that if all of these people chose to not work on the same exact day, everything would crumble. An interesting perspective to be sure. One that has kept me thinking for so many years.

As I have moved through the maze of life, I have often used this perspective to measure people. Is their effort one that is exemplary? Do they go the extra mile every time? What would the world be like if they were not in it? These are questions that I ask about myself as well.

As a Cubber I strive to create an environment where the boys feel like they are "one of the 5,000". It is critical that every boy feel important individually and as a part of the group. As they grow into young men, it helps with their confidence. As they move into adulthood, it will provide a base from which they can build their character. Make sure they feel like one of the 5,000, but first make sure you are in that group as well.

RESPONSIBILITY AND AUTHORITY

During a recent Pack meeting, the boys in Bear Den 7 were especially rowdy. I have become used to this behavior and do allow some latitude during this special time of celebration. There are times when this does get a little too crazy and curbing them is required. At this meeting, the Den Chief took on the task to corral them.

It is difficult to allow boys to fail. We want so much for our kids and it is part of our nature to protect them. During the valiant effort by the Den Chief, I could see that his approach to separating them was going to create more difficulties than the current status. The look on his face was one of absolute despair as I stepped in to create some calm.

When the meeting was over, I could see the look of frustration on the Den Chief's face. As we talked about it, he let me know in no uncertain terms that he felt I was not allowing him to fulfill his role. After some thought I agreed with him. Now, if any of you have a teenager you can imagine the look of bewilderment he had as I accepted the fault. He was almost in shock.

What he helped me realize was that I was not allowing him to do what he was expected to do. Of course I gave him the responsibility to keep the Den in check. That is one of his jobs as a Den Chief. What I had not done was bestow the absolute authority to do it. When the boys from the Den came to me to complain about his actions, I chose to fix it rather than sending them back to their Den Chief.

I had made a huge mistake. What I had done was strip the Den Chief of the respect he deserves. No matter what he is doing (as long as the kids are safe), I need to support him in his efforts. I gave him the responsibility of getting the job done, but I never really gave him the authority to make it happen.

This has changed. The boys in Bear Den 7 now know that their Den Chief is on an EQUAL plane with their Den Leader. If he says it, then it is as good as me saying it. Two marvelous things have happened as a result. First, although the boys have always liked their Den Chief, they now treat him with a greater level of respect. Second, and probably more important, is that he now initiates discussions about his performance. He enjoys reviewing what he did in certain situations and offers a fair evaluation of his efforts. He is also more receptive to alternate approaches that he can use next time.

If you ever give someone the responsibility to complete a task, make sure you bestow upon him the authority to get it done. Having one without the other is a recipe for failure. They will have enough failures on their own without us setting them up for another.

MR. GOULD, CAN I PLAY?

I usually arrive 30 minutes early for Pack meetings. It gives me an opportunity to ensure that the facilities are prepared for the meeting. It also gives me a chance to see the "eager beavers" get there early as well. These boys are special to me because they are showing their interest in Cubbing.

At one of our Pack meetings, we were all set with a little time to spare. One of the Tiger Cubs came to me and asked if he could play. As I inquired as to just what he wanted to do, he was at a loss. I really didn't want them to play tag or dodge ball, as this can be too disruptive, so I offered a suggestion of practicing his thumb wrestling.

He had no idea what I was talking about. After a few minutes of instruction we were heavy into our match. We split the first two and he was successful in defeating me in the championship bout. He was absolutely delighted and excited for more. I sent him to pick on someone else and he came back each time telling me whom he had beaten.

Mostly kids just want to have fun. They want to play games. Now this boy has a new game he can play. His father has reported to me that he now has something to help pass the time with his son when activities of a more physical nature are not appropriate. They can do it in the waiting room at the doctor's office. It is a great time filler when they are waiting for his school bus to arrive. It can even be useful when waiting for the traffic signal to change from red to green.

The next time your child or one of your Cubbies tells you he wants to play, you now have something to offer them that is fun and safe.

PRACTICE MAKES PERFECT? NOT!

Have you ever done the same activity at two different Den meetings? I know that I have. To hear the boys tell it, "We've already done that before.", or "Why do we have to do it again?", or "I did that with my mom or dad." Does any of that sound familiar?

Sometimes it is because part of the Den was not there when we did it the first time. I want to make sure they have an opportunity to complete the assignment. More often it is because they just need to do it again. Having seen or practiced something once does not mean they have a mastery of the skill.

When the boys express their dissatisfaction with the "redo", I ask them some questions about their schoolwork. According to most of the boys, they have answered the problem of "What is 2 times 2?" about a zillion times. They have written their names more than a gazillion times. For my group, the most often word on spelling tests is "their, there, or they're".

After this exchange I solicit their response as to why they have to do this so many times in school. Most of them have the conclusion that they need to practice these things. These third grade boys point out just how many times they have been practicing their multiplication tables this year. They do understand the importance of these things in their school.

Now it is much easier to get them to "redo" some of their Cubbing skills. They see that without practice they will never become good at doing them. The most important facet of this is the way in which we review the material. If it is done the same way over and over they will lose their interest in it.

During one of these repeat performances I inquired as to why we were doing this again. One of these bright fellows said, "Practice makes perfect". They all seemed to groan when this was said. It was as though they had heard this a gazillion times as well. It was obvious that I needed to eliminate this mind set right away.

In our hurry up society we push ourselves to just get it done. It doesn't seem to matter how, just stay focused on completing the task. This approach is not conducive to ensuring a high retention rate of learning. Practice is the key to making sure it sticks. But poor practice is worse than no practice at all. If someone gets the proper result by accident, they really haven't learned it like they should. The practice needs to contain the same elements EVERY time. Equally as important is that the practice session needs to allow sufficient time to practice all these elements.

In our Den we no longer say, "Practice makes perfect." We now say, "Perfect practice makes perfect." Give them the tools, the time, and enough perfect repetitions to reap the rewards of their practice.

TO THE WORLD

Sometimes as we drudge through our daily activities we feel a little insignificant. Whether it is at our work, at home, or some other place, it can happen to any of us. When we are lumped in with the masses, we sort of feel pretty small.

If that is how you have felt, imagine what a 36" to 48" little person feels like. After all, they are usually lumped in with hundreds of other kids in their school. Dozens of kids in their classroom and Pack. They are one in a handful in their family or Den. Sometimes they don't feel very special either.

When I meet a recruit for the first time, I make it a point to teach them the secret Cub Scout handshake. It is my way of sharing something about Cubs with them. It gives us at least one thing that we are both familiar with. I tell them that this is the way we need to greet each other. So when I see them in the halls at school or a Cub meeting, we poke our hands out and give each other that special greeting.

Rarely am I given the opportunity to initiate the action. Usually they come flying at me with a big smile on their face. They are so excited to see someone they recognize and that they know will recognize them back. As time goes by, they get much better at the handshake. You can feel the confidence in their grip. It is a wonderful thing to experience.

When they reach Webelos age, we will change the handshake; however the greeting is still the same. They may not be so bubbly about it; however I still feel it from them. They are special and they appreciate that I am treating them that way. For at least one time in their day, they are made to feel unique and not just part of the group.

Just keep this in mind, "To the world I may be just one person, but to one person I just may be the world".

THE WAY TO A CUB'S HEART

Kids love to eat. Who doesn't? It still amazes me how much better food tastes when it is prepared and eaten outdoors. Watching a young boy really getting into his food is so special when he doesn't have to use his best table manners. It makes me think that I am looking at him at almost a primal level.

One of my first camp outs as a Webelos Den Leader was a learning experience on all fronts. I knew I would make mistakes, so I concentrated on one area to be guaranteed. That was the meals. I just had to make sure there was healthy food they would eat and I had plenty of it. The menu was pretty simple, so there was work for everyone to do as well.

When you only camp out one night, you pretty much have to make the evening meal special. When I asked the boys what they liked to eat, they said pizza. Cheese and pepperoni were the preferred toppings. Now they think that I am going to have these delivered or something. No way. We're camping.

I trusted my training and just knew we could do it. I learned how to make brownies in a cardboard box. Start with a box that holds several packages of copy paper. You know, the one with the lid. Then line it with aluminum foil. This box has now been turned into an oven. I practiced a lot and got quite good at it. I figured if we could bake brownies we could bake anything.

We started with the cheapest rolled biscuits we could find. Rolled them out, put some sauce on them, added toppings and put them in the oven. Let me tell you that these little guys were a little overwhelmed with it all. They recognized all the pizza components. Still, they just couldn't see how this was going to work.

Of course I had already made them at home before the outing. So it was no surprise to me when I lifted the oven to see some great looking pizzas ready to be eaten. Needless to say, these boys had been at it pretty hard all day and they were ready. It really helped that the pizzas looked so good. One of the boys even said they looked like personal pan style.

I had no idea what I had done. These guys loved them. We just couldn't make enough of them fast enough. I figured four each would be stretching it, but I was prepared for 6. It was a good thing that I was prepared. We eventually had to close the kitchen from lack of supplies. They still didn't go hungry because I had cracker barrel (evening snack) planned for as well. But that's another story.

One particular boy had just begun a major growth spurt. As I am a man of somewhat small stature (that means I am short), boys at the Webelos age are beginning to look me eye to eye. I could see that he was truly enjoying his pizza. When I offered him another he requested two. I was honored to honor his request.

We were still making more pizzas for that stray staff person who heard there was pizza out there, when I saw my hungry friend standing next to me. He was obviously happy with what he had consumed so far. But I could see that he wanted more.

It was perfect timing because a new batch was just coming out. When I set the tray of 6 on the table, he asked me if everyone else was finished eating. I said I wasn't sure, but I wanted to know why he asked. He said, "Mr. Gould, these are just about the best pizzas I have ever had. And I'm really hungry. And I think I could eat all of these."

When I pushed them across the table to him and said, "then I think you should try", it was like I had given him the world. I went back to rolling out more dough while we talked. He shared with me many things about his family, friends, and even himself. It was quite an open and frank conversation.

As he finished up his last pizza for a total of nine, that look of happiness had grown to one of total contentment. The look was complete with the sauce on his cheeks, hands, and shirt. This boy had eaten his fill.

We figured we needed some exercise after eating so much, so he helped me clean up a bit. As we were drying our hands and closing up shop, he stuck out his hand in Cub Scout style. When we shook hands he said, "Mr. Gould, thank you for the best meal of my life. I won't every forget it."

I am not certain that he still remembers, but I always will.

LET THEM STAY UP LATE

It is highly recommended that you not allow more than two Cubs sleep in the same tent. This is to help make sure they go to sleep. If you put more than two together, there is a good chance they will feed on each other's excitement. One may fade and doze off, but after awhile the noise from the others will wake him up. Now with a little rest, he can carry the ball until the next one is ready to go.

I try to let the boys choose their tent mate. I don't really want to force relationships but rather let them come naturally as a by-product of the program. There is usually one boy that is the most popular and everyone wants to tent with him. This can cause some trying times. On one particular outing, I could see that they were not going to work this out on their own.

Since every boy has something to offer to the group, I took a chance and decided to put ALL of them in the same tent. I knew it was crowded and there was no doubt it was going to be a late night. It didn't matter, because I had a greater goal to achieve.

They talked well past lights out. It even went on to the wee hours of the morning. I could not be considered trustworthy if I shared any of the specifics of their conversation. Let it suffice to say that it is very interesting when 4th grade boys are talking about girls and their teachers. It was very enlightening and informative for me.

I just couldn't go any more and fell asleep. At 6AM I got up to start getting ready for breakfast. As I came out of my tent I heard movement amongst the boys in their tent. Now, I figured that it must be one of the boys that went to sleep early and it was time for him to get up on his own. I could not have been more wrong.

It was two of the boys that had stayed up all night. In the past these two boys had been like oil and water. They never seemed to mix. Yet here they were yucking it up between themselves. They were having a great time, together, for the first time. It was like music to my ears.

One of these boys has continued on the Scouting trail, while the other has put his focus on other worthwhile areas in his life. Still they remain good friends. They found something in each other that night that meant something to them. To see that friendship being nurtured to this day is indeed worth any lost sleep that they and I may have had that night.

MOM'S CAMPOUT

My fabulous wife was a Den Leader for our older son during his Wolf and Bear years. The boys had been dying to go camping. My wife is quite comfortable with the camping experience. She was all for it, however, we were just going into the winter months and taking the boys out in such conditions could be just miserable.

After soliciting some input from leaders that had gone before us, we decided to have a mom's campout. There would be no adult males present. This was going to be a special time for the boys to bond with their mothers. We chose the month of February, since it would be so close to Valentine's Day. Seemed very appropriate to us.

I know what you are thinking. You doubt if any mother was willing to go camping with their son in the coldest month of the year. Especially when we had just received about 8" of snow. I am happy to report that we had 100% participation from the moms. But, how could that be? It's hard enough to get them to Den meetings, much less have them spend the night out in the cold.

One of the things I learned in training was that every activity has to have some guarantee of success. People still need to work for their accomplishments; we just try to make sure that any effort yields results. Our plan was simple. Make it hard for them to say no to the experience.

We reserved a portion of a local residence camp. They had a wonderful cabin for the boys to stay in that had a nice potbelly stove for heat. The moms would be staying in the HEATED infirmary. It was all set up with bunk beds, a kitchen and even a small lounge area. Since moms are usually cooking most of the meals, we decided to have everyone bring a sack lunch. As for dinner, we brought in pizzas. Breakfast was also delivered to them. We offered them a great selection of pastries along with milk and juice.

Since I was not present (except as the delivery boy), I cannot offer any first hand observations. I have been told that while the boys were out romping in the snow, the ladies had a marvelous time in the cabin. They just sat around the warmth of the stove and shared all kinds of stories with each other.

They shared their evening meal together and sang a few songs before turning in. Two of the moms are trained leaders, so they stayed with the boys. The rest of the moms headed off to their "camp site". I would love to have heard some of the stories they shared that night.

As I arrived the next morning with their breakfast fare, everyone seemed to be in a good mood. Before they departed, I watched as every mom went to my wife to offer their appreciation for the weekend. They all had a great time. More importantly, they had shared a Cubbing experience with their son. Who could ask for more?

DON'T LET THEM DRIVE YOU CRAZY

We are blessed in our district. The winners of each age group from their Pack's pinewood derby gets an opportunity to race their cars against the boys from other Packs. It is indeed a grand event with almost 200 boys participating each year. It is held at a local shopping mall and is quite a recruiting tool.

I make it a point to attend to support the winners of our Pack. It gives me an opportunity to visit with the parents. It also allows me a chance to get to know the boys a little better as well. They are so cute when they win a heat and it is very important to be there when they don't. They need our support when the pendulum is swinging in either direction.

There was some down time during one division, so I took a minute to step outside and get some fresh air. As I stood there, a lady who worked in the mall joined me. She shared some of her experiences with her son when he was in Cubs. Her tales were not far from any of the others that I have been told. She had some great successes and some minor setbacks.

After a bit, she commented that she should get involved again with Brownies or something. Of course, I encouraged this action. There are never enough volunteers in our movement. It has been my experience that those who get involved without a child have a much purer heart. They are truly doing it for the kids and not just their kid.

It was time for me to get back to the action, so I gave her my contact information and made sure she knew she could call me with any questions she might have. Just as I was opening the door, she thanked me for serving the youth and said; "Don't let them drive you crazy". That comment stopped me in my tracks. I spun around and responded to her, "I never let the parents get in the way of us Cubbies having a good time."

ONE HOUR A WEEK

How many times have you had a laugh over this statement? This phrase was and is used as a recruiting tool for leaders. After all, you only have one meeting a week. It lasts for one hour. So, it only takes one hour a week to be a leader.

For anyone that has been a leader for more than one week knows that this just isn't correct. I usually invest more than one hour just getting ready for that one-hour meeting. Of course this doesn't include additional items such as committee meetings, roundtable, Pack meetings, training and on and on. By my calculations it is more like one hour a day.

I challenge you to consider just what program you can be involved in that gives a greater return than Cubbing. If you have a normal sized Den of 8 boys then your investment of 7 hours gives direct impact of 8 hours to these young lads. That means your return on investment yields a 14% gain. Try getting that return at your bank.

In the beginning, I spent some time researching the program. I wanted to understand the best way to accomplish the objectives. Reading handbooks and Pow Wow materials gave me some tremendous insights. The internet has opened up incredible avenues of information that are also helpful. Of greater importance was the counseling I received from other leaders.

Now, my efforts in the Den are a result of that one hour a day. Some days it is just making phone calls. Other days it is practicing the project we will be doing at the next Den meeting. Still others include planning a little further out for an outing of some sort like camping or a field trip. I have come to the realization that I need that one hour a day. If I don't put some focus on the program every day, I sort of go through withdrawals.

Since I serve on the roundtable staff and training team, the Cubbing program does get more of my time. Actually, the leaders get more of my time. One thing that is important to me is that the boys in my Den get good quality time from me. Another important aspect is that I help other leaders get the most of their time. If I can prevent them from making the same mistakes I have made, then I am maximizing their investment.

What counts is not the number of hours you put in, but rather how much good comes from it.

WHAT IS YOUR FIRST NAME?

Outside your Den I imagine most of your Cubbing time is spent with other leaders. We hang with them at roundtables, training events and the like. It is a great way to learn the ways of others while creating bonds that last a lifetime.

Recently, I was at a district wide event. There were leaders from all over the district there and it was a grand sight. As my fortune would have it, several of these leaders were accompanied by their sons. I just love meeting Cubs for the first time. There is no greater feeling than to get down on ones knees and offer that boy the special Cub Scout handshake.

One particular boy that I met was a new Tiger. He looked so good with that orange neckerchief on. It is also interesting to tie the boy to the leader. Sometimes you just don't see the connection; however, with this pair it was quite obvious that his dad had a great influence on him. He was just a kid just like his dad.

We talked about all sorts of things that he likes about Scouts. I made a special point of how much I respected his father. I told him how much I appreciated his father's efforts in Cubbing. The look on his face was one of surprise when I thanked him for letting his dad help other boys and leaders with the program. I'll bet he thought he was the only kid in the world that saw his dad leave the house for "another Scout meeting". He now knew he wasn't alone.

Don't ever believe that you are the one making the sacrifice, because your family is making a greater one. After all, your sons just want to be with you. They can be soured on the program, when they see you leaving them night after night going who knows where. Make sure you invest time with them as well.

I guess my visit with this young lad had some impact. I received a note from his dad telling me how much his son enjoyed our little talk. He thought that I was "cool". Now I am not that cool, but I know his dad is. I believe that is what the boy was impressed with. He finally found someone who understood his position and knew how much he missed his dad when he was gone.

At the end of his note he said he had asked his son what my first name was. He replied, "Mister". What a wonderful sign of showing respect to someone who had showed it to him.

MRS. M.

It has been many, many years since I was a Cubbie. Most of my memories of those days are quite faint. However, many are as vivid as if it had happened yesterday. Especially the fun times. I think that is how the mind works.

My Den Mother was Mrs. M. She had sort of a "one room Den meeting". There were boys of all ages in the group. We had a couple of boys working towards each of the Wolf, Bear, and Lion ranks. Yes, I am that old. I actually earned the rank of Lion before it was set aside for an expanded Webelos program.

We had all kinds of fun. There was always a game and most of the time we made something. I particularly remember taking an apple and sticking it full of whole cloves. It was something you could hang in a closet or some other place that you wanted a special smell. I still have that apple, although it is about the size of a walnut now.

We moved just about the time that I was to go into Boy Scouts so I lost touch with everyone that I knew as a Cub. Now, so many years later, I have truly discovered that Mrs. M. was a very special lady. Not only was she special to me, she was special to many other boys. I know because I have met them and we have had great visits about our time with her.

It is strange how someone can impact our lives without us realizing it. She instilled in me the joy of Cubbing. I had to wait decades for it to become clear that this was her goal. She never had a harsh word to say. She always encouraged us in our efforts. Everything we made was "just beautiful".

Sadly, Mrs. M. is no longer on this planet. I often think she is holding a Den meeting in the sky with a new little brood of kids. I am sure she is encouraging them to "do their best" and has planned her meeting so that it guarantees success for each and every one of them. I am sure she knows how much she helped me and I am anxious to tell her that the next time we meet.

When we do get together again it will be "just beautiful". Thanks Mrs. M.

LIVES ARE CHANGED

As you watch a boy grow up who is in Cubbing, you get to see special things along the way. Most of them are small, seemingly insignificant, events. Still others may be on a grander scale. Usually, it involves just the Cub. Sometimes, there is something that impacts the entire family.

We had a boy show up at a Pack meeting out of the blue one night. He was a first grader so we seated him with the Tigers. He was a bit timid at first. By the end of the meeting, he was reveling in the fun and excitement. He was indeed hooked.

After the meeting, I approached the gentleman that brought him. I commented that it appeared that his son was having a great time and we were excited to have him join our group. Because our society has changed so much since I was a kid, I was not totally surprised when he told me that he was not the boy's father. Instead, he was the live-in boyfriend of the boy's mother.

Well, the boy jumped right in and worked diligently towards his achievement. His mother volunteered for many jobs and was very helpful to our Pack. She continued to comment to me how much her son just loved the program. This was indeed turning into a Scouting family.

After a couple of years, I heard the news that the boy's mother and her boyfriend were going to get married. This was a shock to me, as she had told me on more than one occasion, that she had no plans of ever getting married again. She had given up on the institution of marriage.

After they returned from their honeymoon, I had a chance to visit with her about their trip. She went on and on about how wonderful it was. She also offered how truly happy she was with her new life. I just couldn't resist asking her about previous conversations on the topic of marriage. Her response was overwhelming. She said, "Through Cub Scouts you have been teaching my son great values and we decided that we needed to demonstrate to him that we have values too."

I knew that the program changed boys' lives. Seeing it extend to the entire family was an added bonus that I will never forget.

PEOPLE VALUE THINGS BASED ON WHAT IT COST THEM

Once in a while, we have a boy become involved in the program that comes from a family in need. They may not necessarily be destitute, but rather need to stretch their budget all the time. Our Pack feels an obligation to help them out by waiving our fees whenever possible. Sometimes, it hasn't worked out well. Most of the times, it does.

One particular boy became involved at the Tiger level. He was an absolute gem of a lad. Always with a smile on his face. He truly enjoyed the experience and had a very positive impact on the other boys in his Den. This was a boy who was reaping great rewards by being involved.

When we offer to "scholarship" a boy, we sit down with him and his parents. We explain to them just what they are receiving. It is important that they know the sacrifices that others will make in order for them to participate. Almost without exception, they ask what they can do to help. This family was more than eager to step up.

As with most organizations, we have an annual fundraiser. A portion of their sales is set aside for their own use. Of course, it can only be applied to Cub related expenses like membership or day camp. We have boys that never have an out of pocket expense because their sales are so high. With this particular family, we urged them to participate.

I could see that the boy was excited to help. He asked me many questions about the products. He wanted pointers on just how to sell the items. We even worked together to create a sales "script" from which he worked. When he left our meeting, he said he wanted more than one order form because he knew he could do it.

The sales cycle for our fundraiser lasts about one month. We usually don't know how much the boys are selling until the turn in night. As a result of frequent telephone calls, this boy had kept me up to date with his efforts. He was doing quite well. He kept asking me, "Is this enough?"

This particular year was an incredible success. We had exceeded all of our expectations. As fundraising chair, I was shocked when I discovered the sales totals were 150% of what I predicted. It taught me to never underestimate the power of a group of Cubs.

When I saw the sales from our special boy, I was absolutely blown away. The amount credited to his "account" not only covered his membership fees, but he had enough left over to nearly pay for his summer day camp fees as well. He was the leading salesperson in his Den and was in the top 5 in the Pack. It was indeed a job well done.

If we had just given him his membership, he would not have understood the value of what he was getting. Instead, by "earning" his way, he learned just how much the program was worth. Even at 8 years old, he understood "value". Great lesson from a program that teaches values.

HANG LOOSE

It is an awesome responsibility being a Cub leader. I take it very seriously when a parent leaves their child in my care. This boy is one of the most cherished things in their life. Returning them better than I got them is always my goal. Sometimes, this causes great stress in my life.

During day camp, there is quite a bit of chaos. The boys have more than enough energy to be able to run around during a lull in the action. We try to supply them some items to help pass the time. Frisbees are one great item. Footballs are another. When playtime is over, I feel like a cowboy trying to roundup the cattle for the drive to the next station.

Have you ever noticed that not all the boys calm down at the same time? As you scurry to round up the strays, it is very easy for some of the others to escape from the herd. This is a time that is definitely worth seeing. I'll bet it would be a winner on one of those home video programs. If not, it would still be worth a great laugh.

The level of frustration during these times sort of gets to me. I have been known to let this frustration effect me to the point that I get a little too intense. Recognizing one's faults is always a great place to start. After this acceptance of my weakness, I put together a plan to combat it. I always ask the boys for their help with any task, and this was not going to be an exception.

Young children are very astute. They recognize differences in your personality long before you see it. My request was quite simple. After lunch I sat the boys down and asked them to give me a sign when they thought I was getting "up tight". The sign we chose was holding the thumb and pinky finger in the air. Then, they would simply say, "hang loose, Mr. Gould".

Of course, they all were laughing when they practiced the sign. Something new to put in their bag of tricks. Kids just love to learn new things. Especially if it is from an exotic place like Hawaii. It actually put me in a very good mood to see them having such a good time.

Well, lunchtime was over and we needed to herd them up to move to our first session of the afternoon. Once again the strays were running wildly and that frustration set in. One of the more quiet boys in the group came right up to my face and gave me the sign. As he told me to hang loose in his somewhat meek voice, I couldn't help but laugh.

I put together this master plan of keeping my cool, discussed it with the boys and put the plan in action. Now, less than five minutes after it was implemented, I had already been reminded of it. Kids are so cool. When you ask for help, they are happy to oblige. Several more times during the week, the boys had to give me the sign. It has actually carried over to Den and Pack meetings. This seemingly small act has taken on a great part of my life. I have indeed learned to "hang loose" during times of stress.

MENTAL SCRAP BOOKING

During my Wood Badge training, I was afforded the wonderful experience of having to claim a lost item. When the Senior Patrol Leader held it up, I was pretty sure it wasn't mine. I was not absolutely sure. One thing was definite; it was from someone in my patrol (I'm a barking beaver). I figured that if someone from my patrol was going to be humiliated, it should be a Cubber.

Since a Cubber is always game (still another old term), I threw up my hand and stepped forward. When you are in front of the group at Wood Badge, everything must be said in rhyme. Not sure why they do that, but it sure is fun. I offered the following: "Mr. Senior Patrol Leader, I stand here in absolute shame, For I alone am the one to blame."

He reached out his arm with the precious item. Just as I reached for it he suggested that this transgression required a song. Now most people would just freak out at this point. Not a Cubber. We just love having fun. We're just like a kid anyway. So I immediately kicked off one of my best renditions of the squirrel song.

I knew it was good, because I had such a good time singing it. What I didn't know was how much everyone else enjoyed it. They actually gave me a standing ovation. It was one of the most exhilarating feelings I have had in years. As I walked back to our table, I could see a very sly grin on one of my patrol mates. I sat down next to him and just knew that I could hand him the item. It was his and he knew it. I took the heat for him and it felt great.

Later that day, one of the troop guides asked me if I could teach him the song. I said that I would be happy to do so, if he would sing the song with me during our next weekend together. He agreed, so I quickly scratched down the lyrics and we reviewed the music. He assured me he would be ready when we got back together.

We had a few weeks between our weekend sessions. As I was packing for the return visit, I thought that we could use some props for our squirrel song. My sons just love to buy rabbit pelts. They hang them up in their room like they are Daniel Boone or something. I asked one of them if I could HAVE one of them. The look I received was one of fear, however he finally agreed.

When it was time for us to sing, I pulled out the pelt. I had tied it so that it looked sort of like a squirrel's tale. I tied it onto his back belt loop and he returned the favor with another one I had BORROWED from my son. After our song, another ovation was offered. Great fun.

I shared this story with my son. He told me that he was glad I used his rabbit fur and that he was now part of the story. Reminds me of the saying, "You don't have memories, you make them."

FIRE AND BRIMSTONE

On one campout, we were set up in one of the parent's yards. It was a little cramped but they don't spend much time in camp anyway. Actually, they spent more time in the pool than anything else. It was hot. I mean real hot. Days in the high 90s, nights a balmy 80.

After dinner we hiked down to an old graveyard. Have you ever known a boy who didn't want to go to an old graveyard? It was about a mile, so they were a little tired when they got there. It was indeed my plan for dusk to set in just as we arrived. They read several head stones and of course looked for the oldest dates. As it got darker, I could see they were uneasy, so we headed back.

We had a great campfire. Sang some songs. Saw a couple of skits. Heard several campfire stories. During cracker barrel, I reminded the boys to stay in their tents. I emphasized that if there was a problem, it is important for leaders to know where to find them. One of the guys said it was like the fire escape plan at home. "Absolutely", I replied.

As they headed off to bed, some of them were still talking about the trip to the graveyard. I heard one of them say that it would be cool to do a night hike back there. I stopped them in their tracks. I told them how much I loved night hikes. I wasn't telling them they could go, but I did tell them that if they decided to take off, they had to come ask me to tag along.

They were still up for a while after lights out and I made a trip to the tent to get them to settle down. They did get a little quieter, but they still weren't ready for sleep. After about an hour, they must have figured that their old Den Leader was asleep. They have since learned to listen for the snoring. Anyway, they exited their tents.

This was a big mistake, since I had just reminded them that they needed to stay in there. I figured they would take off on their hike without me. To my surprise they headed for the firebox and I could see they were trying to rekindle the flame that was almost out. I let them struggle for a while, hoping that another leader would catch them.

My tent flap was open, so I could clearly observe their actions. I still cannot figure out how they didn't see me there. When I was fairly certain that I was the only adult awake, I spoke to them in my deepest of voices. "Gentleman, you have two choices. Get in your tent or I am taking you home. It's your choice." They froze in their tracks and sheepishly went to their tents.

The next morning, the host father pulled me aside. He told me he was awake while the boys were messing with the fire. He was going to intercede, but he saw that I was still awake and let me handle it. What was great was that he could see their faces. He said they looked like they were hearing God speak to them. They were really scared. How about that fire and brimstone?

I NEED SOME COUNSEL

As a Tiger Den Coach, I had the pleasure of introducing Cubbing to some wonderful kids and their families. I would start them off by doing a few meetings (sometimes more than a few), and search for that elusive leader. It is not my style to force this role on anyone. When they are ready, they will step forward.

One particular Den was very special to me. I immediately bonded with the boys. They were a raucous group that enjoyed their meetings. Even more, they just enjoyed being together. The parents blended as well. It was a Den family if I ever saw one.

There was a father in the group that had an older Scout that had earned his Eagle. I thought for sure that he would be the one. It was not to be at this time. Another dad was a Life for life. That means he reached the rank of Life before leaving the Scouting program. He is the one that became the Den Leader for the group.

I impress on new leaders that I am there for them. If they need something, all they need to do is contact me. I step back and let them run with it. I pop in once in a while to make sure the boys are safe, having fun and learning something. Every time I was there, it was mission accomplished.

About 2 months into their Wolf year, the Den Leader gave me a call. We exchanged pleasantries and he told me he needed some of my counsel. He continued by telling me that one of the boys in the Den had been diagnosed with cancer. It was very early in the treatment, so he didn't really know what the prognosis was. He asked me how he should tell the other boys.

Now understand that I am close to these boys as well. It seemed like several minutes before I could respond. I was in shock. They didn't cover this in any of my training sessions. I told him that this was indeed the first time for me on this issue. I asked him if he had told his son yet and he said no. He did say that he had already thought how to approach it with his son and felt comfortable with what he was going to say.

I asked him who would be best equipped to explain this to the boys. At first, I thought he was choosing between him and me. After a couple of minutes, he gave me the answer I was expecting. His conclusion was that the parent of each boy should be the one. I agreed. At their next meeting, he got the boys out to play and had a session with the parents.

That was a very special group of boys. I have so many stories to tell about them. Their triumphs and setbacks are just inspirational. But this story is about their leader. He didn't need my counsel. He needed my friendship. We both needed someone to cry with. He was and is a great man. His leadership in this Den was absolutely incredible. I indeed learned from that counseling session, even if it started out the other way around.

BE PREPARED FOR WHAT?

Acting on some great counsel I received from a long time Cubber, I decided to take my Webelos Scouts through a "Scoutmaster conference". Since this leader had gone before me, he saw that the boys were overwhelmed with the advancement process. They were very uncomfortable with the testing that they were given. It was great advice and I acted on it.

As a Scout I went through 6 of these. However, I had never been in on the other side of the table. I asked for and received permission to sit in on a conference with a local troop. It was enlightening to say the least. The boy looked very nervous, which I was happy about. I knew this boy and was saddened when he just didn't perform like I knew he could. He knew the material but just wasn't comfortable when asked to demonstrate it.

I made up an agenda for the meetings. It included all the requirements and some general items as well. It was a little rough for the first few, but I got better with practice. The boys were responding well. I knew they were sharing the experience with the others. That made me happy as well.

To say that these sessions were enjoyable would be an understatement. It is a little rare to visit with a single Scout. Since we have them in a group almost all of the time, it was interesting to see their personalities when it was just them. No games. No showmanship. Just being themselves.

It was also somewhat painful. Since I was the one responsible for teaching them these required skills, there performance was a direct reflection on my work. It was obvious that I had fallen short in some areas. I didn't beat myself up over it. I did my best and knew that I would be blessed to do it better next time.

When I questioned each boy about the motto, every one of them knew that they should Be Prepared. In the Webelos handbook it says that Powell was asked what one should be prepared for. His response, "Why, any old thing." Most of the boys had read their handbook and knew this as well. What this means to me is that you have to be thinking ahead. Consider the possibilities of the upcoming situations and what you might need to do.

This type of mind set allows you to be more relaxed. A situation may come up that is not what you wanted, but at least you may have considered it. You will indeed be more able to deal with it and come up with an acceptable approach. You also need to Be Prepared for some other things as well: joy and despair, happiness and sadness, laughter and tears, exhilaration and frustration. Such is the way of the Den Leader.

THE BARF BROTHERS

Note: I was not present when these events happened. I have heard versions and they are varied. This is my interpretation of just what might have happened based on my knowledge of the boys involved. Those who where there probably won't agree with all the details; however the title of this story is what they will indeed agree on.

I just love to see boys bond with each other. What triggers this may be simple. It may also be complex. It may be during a scheduled session. Or it could be during some relax time. Regardless of the event, it is a special moment in their lives.

I have witnessed many of these incredible milestones. I have seen two boys from opposite ends of the spectrum grow closer together because of a common experience. Many times they are shocked that his buddy was going through the same thing as him. What a great initial building block to solidify their relationship.

Without exception, one of the most enjoyed times during a camp outing is mealtime. They really enjoy snarfing down the vittles. It continues to amaze me how they can make a contest out of anything. I guess that's why eating has become of the boys favorites areas to compete in. Who can eat the most or the fastest?

During an incredible outing, it was time for an afternoon snack. They thought they were having too much fun to take a break. But they knew they would soon run out of gas if they didn't fill the tank. They sat down to cool their heels a bit. The menu consisted of one of my favorites, milk and cookies.

They had more cookies than they could eat. There was enough milk to satisfy twice as many boys. That pile of stuff was just too irresistible for a couple of the boys. They decided to have a contest. Who could consume a set amount the fastest? They set their limits and they were off.

One opinion was that it was a virtual tie. Both of them were claiming victory. They began running around the SMALL, HEATED cabin with their index fingers in the air. They were both declaring to be number one. There was a great debate amongst the other boys as to who was the winner.

As the deliberation continued, one of the contestants was beginning to waiver. Apparently, the newly added stomach contents were beginning to have a contest of their own. He really looked bad and you could see what was coming. As he took a seat and listened to the arguments from each side, it was clear that he had other things to worry about.

Now, the other boy was still heavy into it. There were absolutely no adverse reactions to what he had consumed. From the look in his eye and the tone of his voice, he was ready for a rematch. The thought of doing it again sent his opponent over the edge. I guess his mind told him that if he was going to do this again, he needed to make some room.

Boy, did he make some room. As he began to regurgitate the ENTIRE contents of his stomach, there was no place for the others to escape. They could run away from the physical pieces, but they couldn't get away from that most recognizable smell. The milk odor was especially strong.

Everyone was pretty much grossed out with the magnificent display of vomiting. The boys were busy heading for the furthest away point they could find. Then someone noticed the other contestant out of the corner of their eye. He was beginning to fade as well.

This was going to be a sympathy heave. He gently sat himself down, leaned forward and put his head in his hands. After a minute or so, the second act had begun. Now there was no escape for the others. They were trapped in the middle of this unexpected and undesired contest. Most thought the first boy was done, but seeing his opponent beginning to lose it, started him up again.

After what seemed like an eternity, they were indeed done. From the amount of stuff on the floor, surely there was nothing left for them to get rid of. Now the debate was really on. The boys actually began to argue over who had thrown up the most. They were counting chunks and trying to determine the amount of liquid. What a display of competitiveness.

These two boys had indeed had a bonding experience. I doubt they ever dreamed they would be joined by such a bizarre happening. From that point forward, these two boys have been known as "The Barf Brothers". Those boys who were witnesses will never let them forget it. Neither will I.

THE SECRET OF THE WHITTLING CHIP

When a Cub enters the third grade, he is part of a Bear Den. One of the most looked forward to achievements during that year is earning their whittling chip. First, the boys must learn about knife safety. They also learn about the proper use and care of a pocketknife. In addition, they must whittle something in order to demonstrate their skill.

When I am the instructor for this class, I emphasize the TOOL vs. TOY perspective. I still want them to have fun whittling, but this tool must be respected. Since I have never completed the course without at least one small mishap, they see the dangers involved. It is a little sobering to them when they see blood coming from their finger or one of their friend's fingers.

I choose to have them whittle on soap. It is easier for them to cut through it. Another positive aspect is that they can easily start over should their item becomes unrecognizable. They have created arrowheads, crosses, fleur de lis and of course bears. They get quite good at it by the time they get done.

When I make them take the whittling chip oath, I tell them what will happen if they break one of the rules. One corner of the card is cut off for each infraction. I show them my card, which every Den Leader should carry. Mine has two corners taken off. I lost both of them at the same time. I was using a dull knife, when it slipped and put a small gash in my thumb. One was for the dull knife and one was because I was cutting towards myself.

They are also required to have their card in their possession if they want to use their knife. This is the one that usually gets them. When they are getting ready for an outing where they can use their knife, they get excited about packing all their stuff. That includes making sure their knife is packed in a handy place. However, many of them forget to bring their knife "license" at least once.

Of course, they come to their Den Leader and want to know if they can still whittle. I tell them that without a license they can't operate the machinery. Just like a driver's license for a car. As the look of despair comes to their face, I remind them that they can earn it again. That puts a smile on their face.

So he and I take some time to review the rules. It should only take about 30 seconds to do this, but my sessions last for about 5 minutes. This is one of the few times I get to spend with the boy by himself. I get a chance to catch up on the other things in his life. In particular, I want to know how his schoolwork is going and make sure he is contributing in his family life. It's a great time to bond with the lad in a casual setting.

When I issue him his replacement card, I always cut one of the corners off. When they want to know why, I tell them it is because they didn't have their original. This is to remind them to bring it next time. Rarely do they ever forget it the second time. I believe one boy, that has gone through the reissue process five times, holds the record. I have a very special bond with that boy and I think he likes it that way.

A LAMP IS NOT A GUN

I believe trust is one of the most important things you can have between two people. This is especially important when it comes to our children. At a very young age, I have impressed on my sons that they can talk to me about anything. I want them to feel comfortable that we can handle whatever it is. This is critical when they have done something they shouldn't have done.

As part of this approach, we refer to any negative experience as an accident. In this way they didn't "break it". Instead, it was as a result of an accident. This really takes the heat off of them. It is important that I be consistent with them during this process. I can't lose it with them or that level of trust may be breached.

Once they have revealed the facts of the situation, we have a little talk. The basis for our visit is to determine if the accident was preventable. If that is so, and it almost always is, we put together a plan so we can prevent it the next time. It's a great exercise, and my sons have grown greatly because of it.

I returned home one evening to the ire of my wife. She told me that my oldest had had an accident that he and I needed to discuss. I waited for a bit to see if he would bring it up on his own. Seeing that this wasn't going to happen, I used some open-ended questions to get him to tell me about his day. Eventually, he told me about the accident.

We had one of those tall post lamps in our living room. While watching one of his favorite movies, my son decided that he needed a gun. That lamp would be just perfect. He unplugged it and began to wield it like it was a bazooka or a rifle. Isn't the imagination of kids great? During his battle, the pole literally bent in half.

Without bringing it up, he admitted that it was a preventable accident. He already knew this because he had previously used another item as a gun with similar results. Although we were making progress I felt we needed to focus on the preventable part of the equation. I picked up the lamp and asked him what that thing was. He looked at me like I was an idiot when he said, "Dad, it's a lamp."

"So it is not a gun?" was my question to him. "No, it is not a gun." was his reply. Now the chant around our house is "A lamp is not a gun". This phrase has been used quite often. Whenever one of the boys uses something for some reason other than its design, they are told, "A lamp is not a gun". Sounds pretty weird, but it works for us. When my son is at a Scout function and someone is using the wrong tool for the job, I just love it when I hear him explain his version of "A lamp is not a gun."

THE MASTER STORY TELLER

If you hang around this program long enough, you will meet a master storyteller. It may be a man or a woman. They could be old or young. Whatever their place, you know when you have heard them. They just have a way of spinning the tale so that everyone is interested in what they have to say.

I have heard many stories, told by many people. There is one particular person that has impressed me the most with his wonderful talent. He is a long time leader in the Scouting movement. I was honored to serve on the Cub training staff when he was in charge of it. In fact, I was attending a class and since the instructor didn't show up, he just turned it over to me.

This gentleman, who I will call Fred, has shared many stories in my presence. He knows just how to tell one. He gives some background and then paints a picture that is so real to life, that it is spooky. Some of his stories date so far back that I know he wasn't there. Still, he tells the tale as though he was an eyewitness to the event.

Fred is the main reason I decided to tell my stories. He truly inspired me to document these happenings. It is because of him that I realized just how important these stories are. Since I have started putting these down on paper, I have also come to the conclusion that these stories are important to my children. They need to hear them too.

During a session at Boy Scout camp, I asked Fred if he could come to our camp-site and share some stories for the newer boys. You never have to ask a storyteller twice. They just love to share some history and have some fun with the boys. I set it up with the troop, and as the day arrived, no one was more excited than me to have him come.

When he arrived, he was carrying his patch blanket. Calling it that is much less than what it really is. It is a full sized wool blanket that he has modified so he can actually wear it. There is a hole cut in the center so he can put his head through it. When he holds his arms out, it reveals hundreds of patches from decades of experiences. It is a museum piece to be sure.

After I introduced him to the group, he picked up his blanket and pointed to a very small piece of beadwork. It couldn't have been more than a couple of inches wide. It was obvious that it had been made on a small loom of some sort. He proceeded to tell us the story behind the beadwork. When he wanted to join Cubs, he was interested in the things they could make. This very small piece of beadwork was the first thing he did as a Cub. A great story to be sure.

He continued with other stories. All the boys had to do was point to a patch or some other item and he had a story for it. Now, I am not sure that all of these tales were 100% factual, but they were indeed 100% entertaining. Fred can indeed tell a story and I am blessed to have heard many of them. I look forward to hearing more of them in the future.

IS THIS YOUR CALLING?

I cannot tell you how many times I have asked myself why I got involved as a Cubber. There are times when I just can't see any results from my efforts. My plan seems solid and my objectives are clear. Still, the message just doesn't seem to get across to the boys. It has even made me feel like I have failed them.

The only consolation that always works is that I tell myself that I "did my best". That's all we ask of them and that is all we should ask of ourselves. Our best can only be measured by ourselves. We are the only true judge of our skills and talents. Measuring just how we have utilized them is also our call. After all, who knows us better than ourselves?

There have been moments when I wanted to quit. After a particularly unruly meeting is tough. Having a parent give you a hard time over some trivial event is even worse. I have always felt at my lowest point when the boys tell me that the meeting wasn't fun. The most serious sin that a Den Leader can commit.

When I feel that there is nothing left for me to give, I simply recall one of the positive results from my experiences. It gives me the will and determination to go on. Focusing on the successes is a much healthier way to cope than fretting over the failures. I do want to learn from a less than optimum effort. I just decide not to dwell on it. Learn from it and make it better next time.

As I have more and more experiences with these great kids, the feeling of wanting to quit has become less frequent. Since I have probably done it the wrong way from every possible angle, I have fewer and fewer failures. I have made the same mistake twice, but that is a very rare exception.

This "job" became so much easier when I began to view it as a calling. I indeed possess talents that help in my efforts. I didn't always have them. The necessities of the environment have required that I improve some and develop others. I have even done things that I thought I would never be able to do. I have seen in me just what I want to see in the boys.

So I now consider this Cubber thing to be a calling. It is a gift and a challenge offered to me by my higher power. Failure to act on it would be a sin of omission. Demonstrating to the boys that I have decided to quit would be sending them the wrong message. It is acceptable to fail. It is not acceptable to quit trying.

It would not be possible to attempt to be the best Cubber in the world. It is my goal to be the best Cubber that I can be. Keeping my focus on what can be, rather than what is, gives me the inspiration to continue my efforts. For me, being a Cubber is a great calling, because every calling is great when greatly pursued.

IF IT COMES FROM THE HEART

Our council sponsors a Cub Scout Pow Wow on an annual basis. I refer to this event as Cubber College. It is an opportunity for a leader to refine their knowledge and skills by attending classes with very specific objectives. I have attended many of these as a student and I have had the great fortune of being part of the staff for this wonderful gathering.

One year, I was asked to be the instructor for "Pack Ceremonies and Excitement". They sure know how to pick 'em. No one gets more excited about Pack meetings than me. It is the one time when we can shower the boys with praise for their accomplishments. We also have the obligation to challenge them to do even more and do it even better.

After I opened the class by pointing out the restrooms and fire escape routes, we played a game. There are always some adults who just don't quite understand why we treat them like they are kids. It is those leaders that I make sure get involved. They need to understand just whom this program is for. I may see a scowl on their face when I call on them, but it is always a smile when we are done.

For the detail-oriented person, I review the mechanics of the Pack meeting. We go over the room setup, how to build an agenda, and all the other boring things they want to know about. Do not think that this is an area that I consider lightly. It is important to have structure because kids need that. It is just that I would rather put my focus on the fun stuff.

It is a very important part of someone's life when they receive recognition. However, just what they WANT to be recognized for is different for each and every one of them. Some just want the glory for glory's sake. They love the spotlight. Still, others want to feel special inside. They did something that not everyone has done and it's a personal victory. It is usually the "destination" or the "trip" that is at their core.

Regardless of their motivation, the most important role as the leader is to make it unique for them. They may be on stage with several other boys, but they need one moment that is just for them. That special time when the focus is just on them. I can't be responsible for the actions of the other boys and adults in the room. I can only be responsible for my own actions and I will do my best to make this moment "their" moment.

When I present an award to a boy the first thing I do is get down on my knees. I want to get down to their level. I want them to see me eye to eye. I hand them their award from my left hand to their left hand. As we shake hands in our secret way, I give him a firm squeeze. I have made a physical connection with this wonderful being.

I look at him with a smile on my face and I wait until he does the same. They will always smile if they are being smiled at, especially when you are in control of both of their hands. I call him by his name, pronounced correctly. Then I tell him one thing, "You should be proud of the work you did to EARN this award." At this point I don't care what drives them for recognition. What I am conveying to him is that at least one person sincerely respects and honors his accomplishment.

Now comes bonus time. As I stand, I congratulate the parents in a like manner. I want to see them smile too. They also receive my admiration and respect for their efforts in their son's accomplishment. It's kind of a two for one special. I get to honor them in front of their peers, so they get recognition along with their son.

For me, this is the fun stuff. I can practice a ceremony until I have it word perfect. Or I can make tons of mistakes and maybe even have to start over from the beginning. But when that moment comes for me to touch that boy's life none of the rest of it matters. He has to feel it from me. I want him to KNOW that I really care about HIM.

As I concluded the class, I left them with one thing that I know to be true. "If it comes from the heart, anything you do will work."

PERCEPTION IS REALITY

I was a Cub Scout in the late 50s and early 60s. My older brother had already moved on to Boy Scouts. The only contact I had with his Troop was at their Court Of Honor. I don't remember attending very many of them so they must have had only one or two a year. Similar to many of today's Troops.

My brother was a real character. He was always pulling some sort of prank. He had also been a Cub and I'm certain that part of it never left him. He just loved to have fun. There was never a time when he wasn't up for a game of any sort.

I had no specific knowledge of just what it was that they did in Boy Scouts. Once in a while, I could overhear some of his conversations with Dad. As soon as they realized I was around, the topic usually changed to something else. It all seemed so secret. Maybe my dad was just trying to make it a special experience for his oldest son. Yeah, that must be it.

My brother had been talking about the Court Of Honor for weeks. He was to be part of the opening ceremonies. That was indeed a special part. To be one of those chosen to set the tone for the meeting was very important. He spent a lot of time with his Scout buddies rehearsing their parts. This was, of course, done in total secrecy. I could hear tons of laughter, but really had no idea what it was all about.

The day of the event had finally arrived. I could see my brother was excited; however there was this look on his face that just made me feel like he was up to some mischief. All of us kids were decked out in our Class A uniforms. That included my older brother, and my younger brother and sister who are twins. We must have looked good enough for a Rockwell. Mom and Dad were so proud.

At my brother's request, we arrived early so we could get good seats. I remember that I was on the third row, left side, sitting on the aisle. This is so clear because that is exactly where my brother told me to sit. I just figured this was how it was done. With the oldest younger sibling being first, followed by the others in age order and our parents after that.

We were all asked to stand for the presentation of the colors. I could hear them coming down the aisle. The flags came first followed by four color guards, two abreast. Just as the last one got to my row he tripped over the leg of my chair. Down he went. Screaming the most blood-curdling scream you ever heard.

Then I saw who it was. It was my brother. Lying on the floor, surely having received the greatest injury of his life. He had been hurt before. Some even requiring a trip to the hospital. But I had never seen him like this. I was just certain he was going to die and he tripped over MY CHAIR. I was in a panic.

Just then, several of the other boys ran over to my brother. A couple of the leaders were looking over their shoulders. A classic example of a boy-lead Troop if I ever saw one. They were talking between each other while my brother continued to scream and moan. One of them looked up to the Scoutmaster and said, "He has a broken arm."

This was well before the cell phone. It was even before the option of calling 911. The only thing that could be done was to administer emergency first aid and take him to the hospital. As quick as a flash one of the boys ran off and came back with some small sticks to be used as a splint. Another boy took off his neckerchief and used it to tie it off. When that was done, another had removed his neckerchief and they made a sling.

I was indeed scared for my brother. But as they helped him to his feet and escorted him down the aisle, I felt that he was in good hands. These guys went right to it. Their training had really paid off. They handled a very dangerous situation and probably saved my brothers life.

Just then I realized that my mom and dad were still in their seats. I might have understood it from my dad, but mom's lack of participation was mind-boggling. At least we should be heading for the door to be with my brother. I wondered, "What in the world was going on?"

Then came a sound that I knew very well. It was the laughter of my brother and his buddies. The same laughter that came from those secret practice sessions. They all walked back in and took their places next to the flags. No sling. No splints. I had been duped. It was all a ruse.

I don't believe that I was the only person in the room that believed all of this was real. In fact, I am sure I wasn't, because of the looks on my brother's and sister's faces. My sister was even about to cry. I'm sure some of the parents were taken in as well. This was a well-rehearsed stunt and seemed very real.

For me, it didn't SEEM real, it WAS real. There was not one part of me that didn't believe it was real. My perception of the situation was my reality. My brother did trip, he did break his arm and they did take care of him. As I lay down in bed that night, I just knew that I had to be a Boy Scout. I wanted to be ready for any emergency just in case it was real.

HE NEEDED TO PAY THEM BACK

As I have told you, I am one of three Eagle Scout brothers. Our parents always supported our efforts; however, they were not very involved during the process. They would take us to our meetings and offer some assistance with our achievements. Once in a while, my dad would go on a campout but that was indeed a rarity.

When my older brother received his Eagle, the entire family was proud. Since he was a diabetic, it was difficult for him to work toward advancement consistently. He spent quite a bit of time in hospitals. There were limitations to some types of activities. Remember, that this was over 50 years ago so treatments were much different than they are today.

When we got home and I saw that medal up close, I got excited. He told me he would help me finish the work, so I could get mine. It wasn't long before I received my Eagle, and even a shorter time followed before my younger brother received his. We all sort of pushed each other to finish the race. It was an accomplishment that we could individually be proud of and share in the glory of the other's work.

Most Eagle Scouts become a little less active after receiving Scouting's pinnacle award. My brothers and I were not the exception. We each hung around a year or so afterwards, but eventually we were off to tackle other goals and strive for other achievements.

It was interesting to me that this was about the time my father decided to become involved as a leader. He took several positions within the Troop. He had just taken on the position of Assistant Scoutmaster, when my curiosity got the best of me. I just had to know why he wasn't involved with our Scouting, but now he felt he should be doing it. It just didn't seem fair.

When the time was right, I sat down with my dad and posed him that question. His response was priceless. He told me that Scouting had delivered him three wonderful Eagle Scouts. He admitted that he couldn't have taught us the lessons we had learned through Scouting. He realized that he never could have made us leaders the way Scouting had done it.

He concluded by saying, "I need to pay them back. I may not have helped you with your Scouting, but I have to pay back by helping someone else with theirs." I am so proud of my father. He may not have been my Scout leader, but I am sure for those boys, there are wonderful stories that could be told.

DO YOU LOVE YOUR COUNTRY?

It was our very first campout as a Den. We had planned it for months. We are blessed to have plenty of space on our property to have all the boys and their parents set up their tents. So on September 22nd, 2001 we all gathered for a great time. The boys had lots of fun running through the woods and building their own cooking fires.

I didn't plan many specific activities. Sometimes, when boys go camping, there is so much stuff crammed in that they just don't have time to have any fun on their own. This was pointed out to me by several of the boys in our Den. I have learned to receive counsel from everyone.

Although we were expecting some rain, it didn't damper their spirits. They played like the world would never end. One of the dads brought a rope swing that was a great hit. We set up an area where the boys could shoot slingshots in a safe environment. That was just about as popular.

As darkness fell, the boys cooked up their own hot dogs wrapped in a biscuit. This is commonly known as the outdoor version of pigs in a blanket. I had a special meal for the adults. We gorged ourselves on steak and baked potatoes. Ultimately, we even shared it with the boys.

No campout is complete with a campfire. It was well planned with lots of songs and skits. There were several families that brought out their other children and some friends, just for this part of the weekend. Everyone was having a great time, including me. Campfires are supposed to start strong, with lots of high-powered energy from the songs and skits. As you wind it down, you include things that will have a calming effect on the boys, so they will be ready for bed.

To conclude the campfire, I had planned on a United States flag retirement ceremony. I had witnessed several of these, but had never actually been part of performing one. We had a couple of adults cut the flag into appropriate pieces. Then each boy was given the honor of placing his piece into the fire.

You may have already realized that this campout was less than two weeks after the attack on the World Trade Center. The flag retirement was especially moving when you consider the recent events that shocked our country. There wasn't a dry eye in the group as I read from the script. That, of course, included me.

After the flag had been completely consumed, we sang God Bless America as our closing song. As the boys were devouring the cracker barrel snacks, many of the adults were discussing how moving the flag retirement ceremony was. One of the families had brought a guest from Denmark. He was very quiet, not saying much to anyone. I worked my way around the group so I could have a chance to visit with him.

We talked about the reasons for his visit. He was in the United States as part of a world outreach program associated with his church. When the family he was staying with suggested he go with them to their sons Scout campout, he reluctantly agreed. He knew almost nothing of the movement; however, he had a keen interest in learning more about our culture.

When I asked if he was enjoying his trip, he shared the most interesting perspective. He offered his condolences for the recent tragedy that had fallen on our country. As he continued, he told me of the patriotic events he had witnessed during the past few days. He had concluded that much of this was probably not a deep feeling, but rather a reaction to recent events.

It troubled me somewhat to have to do this, but I told him I agreed with his perspective. I went on to explain that all too often Americans take their freedom for granted. We realize that we live in the most powerful nation in the world, however, we don't often think of the price that has been paid for our freedom.

Then he asked me, "You sure love your country, don't you?" When I replied, "Absolutely", he told me that he could tell by the way we had retired the flag. He admired the respect we showed during the ceremony. He went on to say that it was one of the most moving experiences in his life. I told him that I was happy he had been there to share the moment with us.

As soon as those words came out of my mouth, he held up his hand as though he wanted me to stop speaking. He said that he was the one that had been blessed to be there. The gratitude he shared with me was just incredible. I could sense the complete sincerity of his comments. He concluded by saying, "Keep doing this wonderful work for your youth and NEVER let them forget how great your country really is."

A SCOUT IS COUTEOUS

Now, before you go blaming the publisher or the editor of the book, you need to know that courteous is misspelled for a reason. It is indeed not the first time this has happened and I am sure it won't be the last. You see we all make mistakes. Fortunately, what Cub Scouts experience is so new to them. We are lucky because we can make a mistake in one of our meetings and they probably won't notice.

As boys move into Webelos, they are really beginning to mature. They are beginning to realize their physical strengths. Many become quite adept at their particular sport. In addition, their minds are growing as well. They are very observant and rarely does anything get past them.

To help the Webelos boys learn the Boy Scout Oath and Law, I made up sort of a cheat sheet. When we had our opening we would recite them. I would hold up the card and they could just read it. After a while (usually 4 or 5 meetings) they have it down pretty well. It is real cute when I see them close their eyes and recite it from memory. That's when you know they have it.

Well, with all these new fangled computer things I have gotten quite lazy. I don't proofread things like I should. Even with tools like spell checker things do slip through. That's what happened when I made these up. You guessed it, I misspelled courteous on the Scout Law sheet.

I don't embarrass easily. This was no exception. They caught my error as soon as I raised it up. They were laughing and having a good old time. I apologized for my error and asked them to bear with me this time. Of course they did, pronouncing the word as it was spelled. Thanks guys.

Of course it was my intention to get it corrected before the next meeting. Aren't intentions wonderful? As I brought out the sheets for the next meeting, my memory kicked in and I knew I was in trouble. They once again cooperated fully with a couple of variations this time (coh-te-us and coo-te-us). I guess I didn't mention that I had noticed that their analytical mind was maturing as well.

I did have it fixed for the next meeting. However, it was too late for me to be saved. This was something they were never going to let me forget. One great thing is it is something that most of them have not forgotten as well. When I see them at their Boy Scout meetings reciting the Scout Law, there is a little grin on our faces as we get to the fifth point.

I may be biased, but I believe these boys are some of the most courteous that I have ever met. All of them truly keep this point to the best of their ability. Sometimes, we get so worried about everything being perfect that we can miss the point. Here was an instance where the mistake could not have been more glaring. But it still worked and worked very well.

SHARPER TOOLS

When you first begin as a Den Leader, the requirements for a boy to achieve his rank can seem a little overwhelming. As I went through the first time, I was focused on the specifics of that year. I had not really taken the time to view the entire program. The second time through gave me a different perspective.

Of course, it all seemed familiar. It should because we had done it once before. But there was something more. I knew that because I was beginning to associate the activity to the wrong rank. In other words, I remembered doing something like this at the Bear level but we were only at the Wolf level. This made me take pause to view the activities side by side.

It was so revealing that I included the Tiger and Webelos. What I discovered was that we were essentially doing the same things every year. Now, I realize that many of you will say, "I already knew that". And that is just great. But imagine how excited I was to come to this conclusion.

As we graduate boys from one year to the next, many of the parents will ask me the differences in the ranks. My response is simple; we will do the same kinds of things as last year. This year we will trust them with sharper tools.

IT WORKS, IT REALLY WORKS

There comes a time in every den when the boys' behavior really stretches the limits. They know what the rules are. The consequences have been explained to them as well. Still, they are always testing, just to see how far they can stretch it. If you haven't seen it yet, you will.

We had a great Den meeting following our Blue and Gold Banquet. All the boys were excited to have received their new rank patches. Additional recognition was given to the boys who had completed their religious awards. Beads were being strung on their Den Doodle and snacks were being snarfed like crazy.

Our activity that week was to clean up their Den Leader. I had grown a beard starting at the end of day camp the previous year. So, I let them color my beard and then they got to shave it off. If was great fun from where I was sitting. However, from the looks of the parents, it must have been even funnier from the other side.

This didn't take them very long, as they were somewhat anxious to get outside to play. After the bulk of the whiskers had been whacked off, the Den Chiefs took them outside for a game. I took a few minutes to clean myself up. The parents then got a quick review of upcoming activities. Since the meeting end time was growing close, I went out to gather the flock.

They were of course playing some rough and tumble game. I couldn't quite figure out what it was. There were a few boys sitting on the sidelines looking quite tired. There were others still chasing each other around with reckless abandon. That's when I saw it. A most grievous act. I am sure he wasn't the only one doing it, but he was the one I saw.

You have probably noticed that I speak of safety quite often. I view this as the most important responsibility a Den Leader has. If you cannot keep a boy safe, then you lose his trust and the trust of his parents. What I saw was an unsafe act. A boy threw something at one of the Den Chiefs. Since the boy was my younger son and the Den Chief was my older son, this was not a new sight to me. They had done this before and they both knew that it is wrong.

My reaction was quick and definitive. I got the attention of my younger son and I sent him home with his mother. It breaks my heart to see their heart break, however, the entire Den needed to witness this event. They need to know that there are certain types of behavior that will not be accepted.

As we gathered for our living circle to end the meeting, I made sure that each and every boy in the group knew that their friend was gone. They agreed that what he did was wrong and sending him home was appropriate. We closed our meeting and I packed my stuff to go home.

Sending a boy home from a meeting was not new to me. Fortunately, I have only had to do it one other time. You have probably guessed; it was my older son. I believe he was a year older though. Lessons learned come faster the second time around. It wasn't the same circumstances that caused it, however the result was similar. A heartbroken kid and a group of shocked boys.

Just as we pulled into the driveway I asked my older son if he remembered when he was sent home. "Yes, I do.", was his reply. I asked him why he remembered it so well and he said, "Because it works, it really works."

I JUST LET YOU

My focus for this book is Cubbing. However, it would not be complete unless I gave you some perspective of what my Boy Scout Scoutmaster was like. As an Eagle Scout this becomes even more important. My Scoutmaster had the second greatest male influence on my young life, after my father. Both were fine leaders in their own right.

After my older son's first year of Cubs, I decided to visit the Boy Scout camp of my youth. It was in conjunction with an annual event at the camp. My brother went along with me and we had a great time walking some of the old paths and visiting a few of our "regular" places. I felt like I was a young teenager again. It was fantastic.

As often happens at these outings, we ran into several people from our past. When we mentioned the name of our Scoutmaster, one person told us he was on the reservation and just where we could find him. So off to the maintenance shack we went. Definitely not a surprise location. He was always helping someone.

He recognized us and knew our names. That was very impressive since it had been over 25 years since he had seen us last. We had just a wonderful visit. He recounted many of our escapades, embarrassing or not. He had an excellent memory for detail. It made me feel like we were experiencing it all over again.

Since I was now an adult I was interested in his leadership skills. I wanted to be able to utilize the best of what he did in my own group of boys. I found it fascinating that he never answered any of my questions directly. Rather he would review some options and then ask for my input. Now it was truly déjà vu. This was just like he used to deal with us when we were Senior Patrol Leaders.

Our Troop was extremely good at competitive events. We would often take first place and I can never remember being out of the top 3. We loved to camp and we loved to make our campsites picture perfect. It was difficult at first, but as we gained experience, we got better and better. The best part about it was that it really became quite easy to have a model camp.

For many years I wondered how we did it. I guess the fun of doing it was so great that I had never focused on just how we got it done. That was one of the questions I posed to my Scoutmaster, "Just how did you get us to do all that stuff?" His reply, "I just let you." Thank you, sir, for allowing us to grow.

NOW IT'S YOUR TURN

There is only one more story left to tell. The one that is in YOUR heart. I could never convey to you how much it has meant to me to put these stories down on paper. It has been therapeutic because it has forced me to look at events in my life that changed it. I have laughed many times during the process. I have also cried. Usually tears of joy, but some of sadness.

The important thing is that I have told my stories. Initially, I did it for the money. As it progressed I could feel that it was something more. This has allowed me to leave a legacy. To my children. To the rest of my family. To those boys and adults from which these stories derive.

It has also allowed me to offer hope. One thing is for sure, if I can be a Cubber, then anyone can. I have made more mistakes than you can imagine. I have done the wrong things. I have said the wrong things. I have pushed when I should have pulled. It still worked because throughout it all I maintained the passion for the program.

Although Baden Powell was somewhat of a rascal, he indeed was a genius. He devised a system by which we can instill great values in the youth of any generation. Although it has gone through some changes, the basics remain the same. The great thing is that it has passed the test of time. For nearly 100 years boys have been part of the movement. That's an incredible testament to the power of what Powell created.

I am just a carrier of the torch. I will be here for a short while to keep the fires burning for these very special boys. It is an honor and a privilege to serve in this manner. I know of no better way to invest my time than in Cubs. I once heard that if you are planting for a year, plant rice. If you are planting for decades, plant trees. If you are planting for centuries, plant people.

I challenge you to nurture these wonderful boys. Tend them well and prepare them for the storms they will face as they grow. Give them the courage to weather it all. Impart to them the knowledge and desire to get it done. Above all, love them through the process. Each boy is running his own race. Give him the time to finish on his own.

Finally, I encourage you to tell your own stories. Someone needs to hear them. I am confident there are a lot of people who need to hear them. There will be others who just want to hear them. That's the category I fall into. I want to hear your stories. Basically I want to hear them because I love to hear stories. That's the kid in me.

So tell your stories. Write them down because "someone has to tell the stories" and I think that someone should be you.

978-0-595-39564-4
0-595-39564-3

Made in the USA
Middletown, DE
17 March 2015